Acknowledgements

Previously Published in:

"**Renascence**," *Kentucky Anthology: 200 Years of Writing In the Bluegrass State* (University of Kentucky Press)
Open 24 Hours, Brescia University

"**The Love That Was Missouri**,"
Legal Studies Forum, University of West Virginia

"**Indian Ponies**,"
Open 24 Hours, Brescia University
Love That Moves The Sun (Broadstone Books)

"**The Light In the Distant Room**,"
Open 24 Hours, Brescia University
Kentucky Humanities Council Magazine,
Love That Moves The Sun (Broadstone Books)

"**Snowbound**," *Open 24 Hours*, Brescia University
"**Comes The Last Line Dancing**," *Open 24 Hours*, Brescia University
"**Johnny's Letter**," *Open 24 Hours*, Brescia University
"**Olivia's Letter**," *Open 24 Hours*, Brescia University

Cover art by Mary Belle Taylor (Hay) (1883–1939)
Painted by Mary Belle Taylor in the 1920's, this detail is part of a fresco on the breakfast porch wall at Scotland Farm where she lived, and where it remains today.
Mary Belle Taylor lived as an artist in temperament and skill.

Book Design Marjorie Snelson Design

Printed in the United States

ISBN 978-0-9988211-1-5

For information: johnhay@juno.com
To order: www.createspace.com/8328708

Love's Invisible Language

NOVEL IN STORIES

John Hay

Love's Invisible Language

Backroads apart,
Or on the Seven Seas,
A thought calls
In the field,
Love touches love;
We light up.
A kiss!
Protection!
In love's invisible language
Hearts beat together.

Table of Contents

Snowbound With Julia

At ease, he lolled against the lamppost under the yellow arc light. The street was shiny in the cold. What was going on was not his business, he knew. His ease came from a deeper awareness consciously attained. His trim wool coat was dark and long and warm. His hair was swept back by the wind. It was midnight on the iron clock. The heavy bells of the clock echoed twelve times through the great arches of falling snow, as songs of prayer.

A dozen protestors were rolling about on the sidewalk. They were beating each other with black and white signs on heavy sticks—neat letters, software drawn. It was the women who were beating each other now. The men had dropped their signs and were using fists and feet.

Some signs said "NO" and the others "YES." A tall woman in a black cocktail dress, open red sweater, string of white pearls, came out of the hotel. She stood near Johnny's side, very near his shoulder. Calmly they watched a man lunge from the sidewalk to hit one of the women in the hip with his shoulder. She fell flat with her arms over her head, and the hearing aid she was wearing slid across the ice. Her glasses hung from an ear as she rolled off the low curb like a log. She scrambled to her feet and galloped blindly, headlong into a plump little man who was trying to stay out of it. Regaining his feet, he stepped back, hiked up his jeans, and brushed the slush from the "NO" on his sign.

Most likely the woman was a "YES," Johnny thought, and looked on with compassion.

Out of the dark, with the snow in the air around

them, the police, light on their feet, men and women in blue, were running under the tall, white-barked sycamore trees down a long, white, stone walk.

Johnny turned slightly toward the woman beside him, noticed the white string of pearls under her open coat, and spoke to her in a quiet voice: "Here they come, to protect the people from the people."

The woman at his shoulder looked into Johnny's eyes and narrowed hers. With a slight wrinkle of her nose she seemed to say, "Don't waste my time."

The woman, who was now toying with her pearls, was tall. She was trim, as a woman might be who cared for herself, or a woman who, doing little good for herself, has the genes to hold on for a while. And there was power in that trimness.

She had broad shoulders and fine, white teeth, and she held a slight smile at her lips. Standing there she expressed a confidence, inborn, and boldness forced on her by life. It didn't seem to Johnny that she was the type to slow down to court peace or to learn anything from books; he felt that everything had come to her from the road. His feeling was that she didn't give a damn about many things, yet she was interested, very interested. He noticed she held an open beer hidden under the fold of her coat. He saw her body give slightly forward and slightly back, and he knew it wasn't only the wind that moved her.

"There's a mess," she said. "Yes and No going at it."

They stood together studying what was before them. She was passing by from a night of drinking. Johnny was passing by after five years secluded in the mountains. He had not yet driven out to his home, the nineteenth century farm among the trees. Not yet leaned against Spirit, his calm, white mare, nor chatted softly with Deliberator, the blind thoroughbred stallion. Not yet looked up at the moon hovering there, the moon of his youth. Not yet embraced his mother whom he had been told by phone was sleeping. He had just rolled into town on the empty back road in a very old, battered, red, Lincoln Continental. He was attracted to the crowd in front of the hotel. Always inclined to study his culture, he pulled over.

He and the woman in the black dress and pearls stood together with similar attitudes of detachment, each of them with that inborn grasp of this human struggle on the ice before them, each of them with a healthy and truthful distance from it—the woman with a restless edge, an erratic inwardness ready to do its own damage somewhere else; and Johnny with a deeper presence, a state of being he had worked for.

I'm not going to engage this woman, Johnny thought. She looks at me for a few, long seconds. I don't look back. She wants something now. Her body sways. She sways as if giving in to alcohol and the wind, which seem a relief for her, maybe from standing firm in so much else in her life, with no relief but chemicals and the aberrant winds.

The police wrestled fighters to the ground. Two young women in jeans and stylish boots from a hiking store were screaming at the police. The tall woman and Johnny were calm, interested and calm, but in very different ways. A large earring slid across the ice to the tall woman's feet. The woman in pearls put a foot on it and slid it back across the ice between the legs of a man in a sweatshirt and brown toboggan cap. Johnny looked at her; she was smiling slightly, amused, not taken in by any of it.

“This is boring,” she said to Johnny. “Who are you?”

“I’m Johnny.”

“Well, good for you,” she quipped. “I’m Julia. Who’s he?”

“I grew up on a farm up the road.”

“Well, good for you again,” she said. She tried to focus her eyes hard on him. “I’m the girl next door, who will never invite you over. Got a car?”

“Yeah, I have a car. Lots of windows, a few doors.” Johnny had picked up her mood and was entering in.

“Right, cars have windows and doors,” she shot back. “How about wheels?”

“Yeah, wheels,” Johnny said.

“Well, Farm Boy, Johnny, whatever your name is, my truck left me with a son-of-a-bitch at the wheel. Thinks he rules the world. How about a ride to the Midland Tavern.”

“Tavern?” Johnny knew the place.

“Wake up, Farm Boy. How many taverns are there in this ruin?”

“Oh yeah, that one. I know it. I can see it from the roof of my house over the trees.”

“Over the trees? Must be a tall house.”

“Midland Tavern. Used to pass it every day.”

“Why pass it? Where’s your car?”

Johnny liked the woman very much. He knew she felt comfortable to be tough on him. He knew she felt safe because she recognized his extreme flexibility each time she pressed him, and she felt he would not hurt her feelings. He could tell that she had been hurt a lot, and that she could tell that he did not care to hurt her. She felt his sympathy and his caring, yet she did not know what it was; she felt it as a lioness might feel the safety of nightfall.

The police soon dispersed the protestors, and then jogged back under the white sycamores in their blue jackets for another call to trouble. A frail janitor with a wooden cane walked tentatively from the hotel onto the frigid pavement in the silence of the snow swirling. The light wind made him shiver in his thin coat as he bent down and placed a container of plastic garbage bags on the ice. He began slowly to stack the abandoned signs, very slowly because he was weak, and he began to pick up what the protestors had left on the ground: paper cups, cigarette butts, crushed doughnuts, a scattered cake, a lipstick, and yesterday's papers that fluttered headlines in the breeze.

Johnny and the woman moved in quickly and pulled plastic bags from the box. Johnny saw the woman work hard and quick at picking up the trash, unconcerned with the grime. There was strength and capacity in her tremendous focus; there was a blessing hidden in her work.

The woman kicked red ice into the street where someone had bled profusely from the nose. "Good luck," she said to the absent owner of the blood. "You'll need it."

In five minutes the three of them had cleaned the area. They left the bags by the door where the janitor pointed. Still shivering, the frail man thanked them quietly with gracious emotion.

Side by side, focused and quiet, Johnny and the woman knelt at the concrete curb and cleaned their hands in the fresh snow. Snow cushioned their knees. She pulled up her dress to kneel and did not mind the wet from the snow. There was a feeling of prayer between them in the quiet, and both of them knew it; kneeling together in silence at the curb, smoothing the snow over their hands and seeing it melt; and as they stood up slowly they met each other's eyes as if there had been a tremendous break of peace in the run of the night: kneeling together in the snow, without words, and being finished with what went before.

They walked together in the direction of his car. She thought of Rick, who had taken her truck; and the thought hurt her. She shook off that peace. She shook off silence.

"You're an idiot," she told Johnny. "Now, do you feel good about yourself, Garbage Man?

Johnny felt nothing about helping the frail janitor. He grew up on the farm, and there, with his family, you always lent a hand. It was understood to do it and forget it, not to give credit to one's self. He knew she was like that, too. He could feel it from her. She seemed to be hurting from something else.

"I needed the exercise," Johnny said. "I've been driving since early morning." She answered him with a nod.

She felt he would do her bidding. She didn't reflect on it in her mind; she just felt he was there to help her. He was an apparition who appeared from heaven, who understood, held her rhythms. He was to her, at that moment, like an angel who could not refuse her, a shadow at her side while she solved the problems of the night. He was just a dream. She didn't think about why he had blended with her; she just kept moving, and his presence made her feel secure, free to create.

The red Lincoln was covered with snow. The car was from an era gone by. It was old and battered from much time on the roads. On the back was a continental kit that held the tire. He had bought the car for a song when he lived in the mountains in a time of meditation, and he drove it very little then.

The woman brushed snow from the windshield and the hood with her bare hand. "You ever thought about fixing these dents, Farm Boy?"

"Now and then," Johnny said.

She stepped back in the dark night under the white sycamore, and the snow fell around her. It was catching in her hair and eyelids, and she brushed it away from her face. She looked at Johnny, feeling his presence. All was still and quiet around them with the soft snow falling. She took a long drink from the beer and, looking at Johnny, said, "Naw," with a wry smile. She jerked twice at the door handle, cursed it, and got in laughing.

She tossed the empty beer can to the floorboard, gave it a kick, and pulled a fresh one from her coat pocket. She popped the top, and the beer spewed on her and the car seat. She ignored it. Her fingers were long and restless. In the car's dome light, her eyes were emerald green. Her high cheekbones glistened.

"What the hell do you do?" she asked, laughing. She brushed the beer from her chest and buttoned her low-cut red sweater, which read, "I'm in Love with Rumi." A heart was emblazoned on it and a Rumi figure smoothly spinning in a web of green and gold glitter. She saw Johnny lean to read it.

"Thrift shop," she said. "I don't know the man."

"Poet," Johnny said.

"Good for him."

All of that and pearls, too, Johnny thought, pure, white, simple, full of light, beautiful pearls, a symbol, a reminder… cool pearls against her warmth. And she knows the man more than she knows.

"So where are you going?" she asked again.

"Tonight? Not sure," he told her.

"Liar," she shot back. "Nowhere is fine. Somewhere, nowhere, then you die."

She looked out the window and rolled it slowly down to look at the flash of the snow; she imagined a new moon in spring setting like a sliver of ice.

She lit a cigarette. "Nice night," she said softly.

"Yeah," Johnny said. "It is." He spoke as she had spoken.

Then something else came through, as if she could not stand that ease of feeling, the ease of snow, the frosted windows, the drive through the night

"That son-of-a-bitch would block out the sun," she said.

Johnny knew that they were on their way to find her truck and the son-of-a-bitch. "Do you want to find him?" he asked quietly.

"Yeah, we'll find him. Hang a right. Quick. There! What's wrong, still learning to drive?" She laughed happily and took a drink from the can.

They drove through a dark neighborhood with very small brick houses and a few young trees and a few old ones now and then across a yard. The houses had low porches and small back yards with iron swings and storage buildings and tethered dogs.

"Stop," she said. "Hold this." She handed Johnny her cigarette and her can of beer, got out, slammed the heavy door and swept up to the small picture window of the little brick house. She peered in, then pushed herself away from the glass with both hands, spun away like a dancer, and stepped on to the low porch. She shook the handle of the door.

Locked. She slammed the storm door shut with a hard backhand, and the glass cracked and shattered to the concrete floor of the porch.

There was a small, stone urn sitting on a stand by the sidewalk. Gargoyles decorated its edges. She turned smoothly and with one leg straight out, in a move that spoke of training, tipped it with a flick of her foot, like picking a flower, and it crashed to the sidewalk and broke into three pieces.

Getting in the car, she closed the door gently, carefully removed the beer and the cigarette from Johnny's hands, took a long drink and spoke calmly.

"He wasn't home. Let's go."

Johnny was not moved one way or the other by her anger. He was learning about her.

She watched him. "You want a drink of my beer," she asked. "Sorry. I was rude not to offer sooner."

Johnny spoke gently. "No thanks."

The snow had not stopped. The night felt sharp and clear and dark and friendly with the snow rushing against the windshield.

Johnny suddenly had a feeling of Deya', a stone village in the mountains on an island in the Mediterranean where he had lived. He thought about the sea there, and going to the sea with his loved one.

Olivia would pack a breakfast for them of fruit and bread and cheese and tomatoes, and they would go early before the sunrise to watch the day begin over the sea.

He and Olivia would choose the high cliff above the sea. She lived as beauty, and Johnny loved her and felt her to be as beautiful as a rare bird in a jungle, a human bird, singing. And tonight, years later, he loved Julia as a rare bird in a jungle, singing a different song from Olivia's, and yet, the same song—the hymn of love seeking love.

"Do you like to swim?" Johnny asked Julia.

"I can swim," she said. "Why? Do you think I would look good in a bathing suit?"

Johnny smiled.

Johnny knew that her thoughts about her truck and the son-of-a-bitch were mixing into her conversation with him, her emotions toward the man in the truck clinging to her. "No, I wasn't thinking that," he said. "I was thinking of a place I used to swim."

"Where was it?"

"A calla in the Mediterranean."

"Speak English," she said sharply. "Life is short."

"A cove."

"Good for you; you know what a cove is. Maybe you have a life somewhere after all." Then her voice became warm, tender, reflecting ease. "We have a cove on the river here," she said, "a good place to lay out, get sun. Quiet there. I go alone. Sometimes I swim. Yet it doesn't seem fresh and clean enough for me. It is missing something."

"Missing something?"

"Wake up, Farm Boy. Missing means that something that should be there is not. Get it?"

Johnny smiled and nodded. She moved her hands like birds shifting in flight; she would turn in the seat and lift her head, and her eyes would graze over Johnny. Looking into the woods and into the dark side roads, watching for her truck, she was focused, a lioness hunting.

"No tracks in the snow," she said. "If that bastard pulled off onto one of his favorite parking places, I will see the tracks. Slow down."

She scanned the dark empty yard of a small farm.

"That woman isn't home either, if you can call an idiot a woman. If I find them together, he's finished."

Johnny was listening to her carefully, and he would remember. He had seen her brilliance in the space between the words, in her movements, in the timber of her voice, in her leanings toward a radical adjustment within. Julia's scattered forces brought a vision of Olivia, focused, at ease. It was Christmas morning on the island of Mallorca off Spain in the stone village of Deya'.

He and Olivia were sitting close against the open fire—an olive wood fire—shoulders touching. Walking far from his home at the foot of the mountain, on that Christmas morning, in the cold bluster of wind and ice, a friend, the poet, Robert Graves, brought a gift—his rendition of Omar Khayyam's *Rubaiyat*, and sat with them by the fire. When their friend had gone, they read the poems and felt all the great mysteries, in a different way, intimate, of the moment; and they felt secure in the knowledge—embraced by the warmth of the open fire—that their utmost venture in life was to solve those mysteries. Later in the night, under her pillow, Johnny left a poem for Olivia, feeling her loveliness, in the manner of Khayyam.

Oh my Sweetheart, the burning Stars are bright.
Love calls like Wine hidden in the Night.
Our countless Kisses, the vagrant Rose,
Sing for us their Songs of Light.

Johnny wished all that beauty someday for Julia, as she road beside him, restless and new in her search for it.

Julia and Johnny rolled in slowly and quietly, in the old, red Lincoln with its dents and rumble, past the dark cedars, into the crossroad lit dimly by arc lights. Only a handful of houses surrounded the empty crossroad, and no light was on. There were only a few white houses and a wooden grocery where an antique gas pump stood—a tall robot with a golden face, erect in the falling snow. The houses were dark, the people in them sleeping. It was a wide and rough four-way stop, all gravel and snow and empty trees. In the emptiness and the dampness and the snow freezing at the edges of the road, the motor rumbled. Then, out of the black curve a red pick-up truck rolled in slowly—big, solid—the red shine suddenly brighter as it moved under the arc light. Julia's truck. It stopped in the part of the crossing to the right of Johnny's red Lincoln. Johnny accelerated and rolled out into the center of the intersection, the first tracks in new snow.

Julia grasped Johnny's arm tightly as if she were falling. "Stop the car," she said. "Stop the damn car."

The Lincoln, shining in the arc lights in the swirl of snow, came to a stop at dead center where the four roads made the cross.

Julia put her hand out, opened the door, then slammed it shut, sinking back into the seat, as if she were giving up, surrendering to something for the first time in her life. She turned her head against the seat toward Johnny, as someone might turn their head for a gentle kiss. She searched for his eyes.

"Okay Farm Boy, you win, Johnny, whatever your name is, I've fallen in love with you. You are a strange one. It has always taken me months to half love some idiot man. Maybe it's the way you pick up garbage." She laughed softly. She touched her eyes. Tears were welling up. "Maybe it's the way you have looked at me, like you loved me. Maybe it is just being near you in the car. My life felt different tonight in your car."

"I love you, also," Johnny said, speaking truly, not just for her. "You give to me more than you know."

Julia pulled at the handle of the door then pushed the door open hard with her foot.

"Forget it Farm Boy. I've got things to do. I'll never see you again. I've got a life to unravel, warped as it is. Goodbye Garbage Man. Sweet dreams."

Julia jumped out and bounded across the snow. With a calm sideways jerk of her hand she splashed beer from the can she held onto the windshield of the truck. A gold bracelet at her wrist flashed. The wipers came on in the red truck, a quick answer from the man inside. She jerked open the door and grabbed the man by the arm and tried to pull him from the truck. She was cursing. She was talking fast, and Johnny rolled down his window to hear.

"Never again, you are mean, you are nothing, nothing." In her smooth, deep voice she breathed fire as cold as ice. "Get out. Get out of my truck, both of you."

The young man resisted, and Johnny could see him in the lights smiling at her contemptuously. He had a dark complexion, big arms, no coat, sleeves rolled up to his biceps. Julia drew back and swung with a level fist, another sign of her training, but the man caught her fist in midair. She jerked away, walked quickly around the hood of the truck, snapped open the passenger door and told the girl to get out. The young woman got out quickly. The girl wore jeans and a tight green t-shirt and a necklace with a green stone that flashed in the headlights. Her coat was in her hand. Almost as tall as Julia in her high-heeled cowboy boots, she stood nonchalantly in the snow, and looked to see what was around her, calm and alert.

Julia held the woman gently by the arm and pointed to Johnny in the Lincoln. The Lincoln and the big truck stood idling, rumbling heavily in the quiet night, both drivers were just waiting in the wings for their cue to move, their focus on Julia.

The girl stepped away from the truck. She seemed confused about what she should do. She hesitated. She looked toward Johnny's car. Julia swung into the truck effortlessly, rolled down her window, and flipped her cigarette high in the air and the sparks trailed. The truck sat for a moment with its engine racing, and then with squealing tires cutting through the snow the red truck fishtailed around Johnny's car and was gone.

A light went on in a nearby house, a door opened. "What's going on out there?"

The girl, who had been standing frozen under the arc light, ran to Johnny's car. She slipped once in her high boots, caught herself with ease, and slid to a stop in the wet snow. Johnny leaned across the seat, pushed open the door for her, and she flowed gracefully in.

"Hello," Johnny said in a quiet, welcoming voice, smiling at her.

"Sorry to intrude," she said. "When you are left at an intersection, sometimes there are not many choices."

She introduced herself as Justine. Then she was quiet. Johnny didn't know where he was, and when Justine said nothing, he let the Lincoln idle there, waiting.

"Are you upset?" he asked.

"Not really," she said, matter-of-factly. "Why be upset? That was Julia. I know her. I know her ways. You don't mind taking me to my car, do you? It's at the Midland Tavern."

Another one, Johnny thought, two people in one

night at lose ends, each with the rare force of detachment. Justine, quiet in her perception, Julia in action—both hailing that night from a tavern, both giving off a bright wine—the tavern of the soul, Johnny thought.

"What kind of car is this?" Justine asked.

"I thought you were going to ask who I am or why I was with your friend. And you are just sitting there quietly asking about a piece of junk."

"You'll tell me the rest," Justine said. "Or I'll find out soon enough. Julia told me just now that you are all right. She gets people right some of the time. I see in you that I could trust her tonight."

"It's a Lincoln."

"Oh really? First one I've been inside. My mother says I am a cousin to Abraham Lincoln. He was funny. She told me his jokes. She said his stories teach you not to believe everything you hear. Kind of a rough connection to make, but it's a start. Who are you?"

"On my way home from a long trip. I live out in Jett on the farm with a little fishing pond out front."

"I know who you are," she said brightly, turning to him. "You're Johnny Reins! My father did some carpentry work for your mother on that farm. He took me with him one day. I remember the fullness of the trees. I can't believe it's you. I was changed there. I was a little girl, maybe eight. Your mother gave me a woven bracelet, red and green and sky blue. She told me that her guardian angel was a little Indian girl. I still wear the bracelet for good luck. Here it is."

Johnny touched it.

"It is soft," she continued. "And I think of her. She played the piano for me and sang for me a happy old song, "I Can't Give You Anything But Love," and encouraged me to dance, and I was not afraid or shy with her, so I danced. I've been dancing ever since. She was a mysterious person, loving. How is she? Tell her hello."

"She's very sick. They say she is dying. I'm on my way home. I called and spoke with a night nurse. She's sleeping. I was asked not to arrive home so late and wake her."

"I'm sorry your mom isn't well. That day I was with her we went up the long, high staircase to the attic to look out over the farm from the roof, and there were shadows on the stairs. I was nervous. I asked if there were ghosts there. She laughed playfully and said, 'Only Ghost Toasties.' And my fear just vanished. You are lucky to have such a mother."

"You saw her as I have always seen her," Johnny said. "She is a great teacher; she always loves. She always gives."

Suddenly the police were behind them, and in bursts and waves pastel light spread over them, revolving on and on. A white police cruiser nosed down, rocked on its springs. The two officers swung out on both sides of the car, flashlights blazed in. The officer on Justine's side called out, "Relax, it's Justine." The other officer asked Johnny for his license. "New Mexico?" What are you doing out here parked in the middle of an intersection?"

Justine leaned into Johnny and spoke, "We were...." "Let him talk," the officer said. The officer was a young woman of medium height with a smooth, youthful face.

"Well," Johnny said, "I've spent a little time in the west, and I just drove home, and I met this woman who asked me for a ride."

Justine interrupted again. She moved across the seat against Johnny, her arm around his shoulders. She leaned against the steering wheel. Johnny noticed that her hair smelled of hyacinths. "Listen Sandy," Justine said. "Julia and I were going to see a movie. I borrowed her truck and we lost touch, and Johnny here was giving her a ride to look for me. We met here by chance, and it's late, and she took her truck to go home, and Johnny is going to drive me to my car at the tavern."

"Why didn't you go on with Julia?"

"Well, I used to know Johnny's mother, so I stayed with him to talk."

"How was Julia?" the officer called Sandy asked, probing. "Was she okay?"

"She was fine. Okay. She is turning over a new leaf, no kidding." Justine's voice wavered. She touched her hair.

"Then why was she pouring beer on her truck and taking a swing at the driver. Was that Rick? Neighbors called in, told us. Did you see drugs?"

"Let me talk to Justine," the other officer said without emotion. He opened the passenger door and sat on the edge of the seat. Justine turned and remained pressed against Johnny. Calmly, the officer looked at Justine and sighed as if he were about to fight a losing battle. The red and blue lights from the cruiser flashed in Justine's eyes.

The officer spoke quietly. He was at ease and very polite, and spoke to Justine as if talking to a child.

"Julia is no good now, Justine," the officer said. "She is going to die or go to jail, and I don't want you with her when she does. Don't excuse her. All people like her have an excuse. Someone pulls them down. They pull someone else down on and on, all into the same hole. I can't help you if you are with her when she goes, or if you take up her habits." Justine turned her head to Johnny, very close, and met his eyes as if to find comfort there. She quickly turned back to the officer.

"Shut up, Jimmy," Justine said to the officer. "You've got Julia all wrong."

He was quiet for a moment, unruffled. "Do you know this man?"

"We just met. Dad worked for his family. I know his mother."

"Get out of the car, Justine," he said. "I'm driving you home."

"Okay, I'll get out, but I'm aware that I don't have to get out. I don't have to do what you tell me, Jimmy. Give me a minute to tell Johnny goodbye."

The other officer, the woman, Sandy, handed Johnny his license, and looked at him carefully. "Haven't seen this car around," she said.

Johnny spoke politely. "No you haven't. I've been away studying. Sorry to cause you this trouble."

The officers went back to the cruiser. Johnny watched them in his mirror. The flashing lights went dark. And again, the peace and silence of a winter night came sifting back; heavy flakes of snow drifted from the sky and settled on the hood of the car.

"Goodbye Johnny," Justine said. "Thank you. Sorry for the trouble."

"Why do you protect Julia?" Johnny spoke quietly and with familiarity, as if he and Justine were long-time friends; he felt that depth between them because of Julia.

"I like her. She is my friend." Justine said. "I want her to live."

"Yeah," Johnny said, and he studied her eyes. "And why is that policeman taking you home?"

"He's my brother," Justine said.

Into Johnny's thoughts came London, Memphis, Asia, a slow drizzle in the Mediterranean, his small town—

everywhere, he thought, people dying in life, asleep, because there exists an inner knowledge they do not seek.

"I, too, want Julia to live," Johnny said.

"You don't know her,"

"Yes, I do. I know her. I know Julia." His voice was clear, direct. "She is a teacher in the wrong school. She knows nothing of her brilliance."

"Thank you, Johnny, whoever you are. I wish someone like you were close to her. She is going down that old road, isn't she, that easy road, the killer road."

"She will change in a heart beat," Johnny said. "She will learn it all while laughing."

"She likes to laugh."

Justine clicked the door shut, and in moments the big cruiser made a long, quiet U-turn across the empty blacktop garlanded with cedars, dusted with snow, the cedars winking on and then off again green in the headlights, and Justine was gone.

Johnny sat alone. He watched the snow falling in big, wet flakes, and watched the silhouettes of the trees rocking back and forth against the sky. He leaned back and thought of his mother, Julia, Justine, Rick and the frail janitor and the policemen, as if they had gathered in a room together with the bright seeing of the wise. As if they had earned a perception so deep that they understood themselves, and so all of humanity. Johnny remembered the protestors trying to inoculate others with their signs of YES and NO. He remembered Omar Khayyam eight hundred years gone by speaking in poetry, telling us with whom awareness is kept:

The Ball no question makes of Ayes and Noes,
But Here or There as strikes the Player goes,

And She that tossed you down into the Field,
She knows about it all—She knows—She knows!

'She' was originally 'He' in the ancient poem," Johnny knew. "Yet no division ultimately; they are together when you speak of the all- encompassing force; I prefer 'She,'" he thought. 'She' can sound more tender." With that, Johnny popped the clutch and the red Lincoln lifted as if on air, like a huge, wide, billowing bird, and snow and gravel flew up toward the night sky, and the tires cut to the black top and squealed, with Johnny shifting smoothly, winding out the gears into the last jump forward, then sailing.

The intersection is empty, Johnny thought, lazy and empty, and all the ones who are driven to seek and find have much to do, and have gone hunting. Lights are off in the little houses. "What's going on out there?"

If you find yourself standing in the empty intersection, Johnny thought, and you are alone, and it is quiet at the crossroads and very empty, it is because Julia, Justine and I have gone, gone on that special road; and some others are on the road, too, those driven toward the knowledge of the self. Maybe they are in big, red, pickup trucks; battered, red Lincolns; great green touring cars, or on foot, not far away, hidden in the crowd.

Find them, they are searching for the keeper of awareness.

Comes the Last Line Dancing
Olivia, Julia, Johnny, Mike

Tonight as always we are flying out, Johnny and I, intending to land in the same country, and so far it has been true. And our home will always be what we have made of its treasures: its people and its roads. What gifted us to use light so? Pass now in metaphor beyond words; in action the answer.

The streets still glistened with the rain of springtime, and if you looked up to the shine of the street lamps or the stars and made sure not to think, timelessness would flow to you, and with your breath any contentment you have earned. That home was the only home that was yours growing up, and you always remember using it to understand people and their circumstance, and it was also the night sky in the moonlight and the love poems you whispered in all kinds of weather.

You remember the doorways where you stamped the wet snow from your boots, and always on the other side you found something or someone to teach you all the things you were learning as you were growing up, and from the high wooden post against the fields, or from the spires of the old church, bells would sing, and the sharp wind and the snow would not be cold at all.

"Olivia," Johnny said to me. "Let's walk around downtown, have dinner at Carmello's. What do you think?"

"Sure," I tell him. "Let's go."

We drove the winding road to town in his battered Lincoln. The glow in the eyes of the animals that watched us go by were there for our delight and to tell us what the earth is like, from what dark caverns of thought its people come. We say it was the divine force that made those hungry eyes and the peace of the back roads, too.

We parked high in the long slope of the alley.

Walking down the alley we held tightly to each other and enjoyed the cold. It was snowing again, big flakes curving in slowly and melting against our lips and cheeks.

We saw a man come fast out of the art gallery with his head down. He missed the curb, slipped in the snow and fell backward into the street. He was a middle-aged man and was quickly up and away, as if he were escaping on the run. "The snow cushioned him," Johnny said.

We stopped at the window looking into the gallery where the paintings were lining the walls. The window was huge and framed the small room. There must have been thirty people there. They were talking, but we could not hear them. No sound came through the thick glass to us in the street. A blue car came down the alley in the snow. A yellow cat leaned against my leg and spun away. A brief burst of wind made the snow tumble in the air. The people in the gallery were talking. In these moments, no one was looking at the paintings lining the walls. The paintings were easy going with saffron trees and orange hills and a brush stroke making an entire mountain, and black and white spotted cattle standing by a river, and an abstract or two in green and gold engaging us. A severe energy had taken over everyone in the room, and people were talking in pairs. Their eyes were stressed by something, and their eyes looked somewhat dead, and they leaned toward each other to hear over the din of voices. The eyes were glazed as if struggling with some sort of loss. Two women and a man had no one to talk to and were standing with their backs to the paintings as if they were glued to the floor.

The paintings hung there as artifacts of the night. The artist was floating in the back of the crowd. We knew the artist. She had put herself into her paintings; she related to them as a part of her being, and she wanted the paintings to be loved. I hoped she would sell all of them, and they would spread out and do what they were meant to do. Someone began to talk to her. They laughed, shook hands and parted, and the artist was alone again.

The owner of the gallery, an artist, too, was sitting in the corner. No one seemed to notice her sitting there. She was leaning with her arm around a child, a boy of about seven. She was looking through the crowd as if it were merely a crowd, and she held the little boy close, who needed her now, who needed her the most.

Johnny and I turned away at ease, and I took his arm in mine.

"Art is what it is," I said. "And it does only what it can do." Johnny smiled and pulled me closer.

"Maybe all the talk keeps it coming," he said.

"We're talking, too," I said.

"I would talk to you forever."

"About art?"

"Only the good in it." Johnny swept his arm through the falling snow and opened his hand out just for the fun of it, as if he were coaxing a little bird to light.

We heard a voice and then another. We turned the corner. There were several people standing on the sidewalk in the cold in front of the wine shop. Through the window we could see a large crowd packed in. There was a woman we knew standing by the long window, and she saw us and stepped out. She was wearing only a sweater, and she had a glass of red wine in her hand. The wine shop was packed with people, and they were all talking loudly. We could not hear them after Martha closed the door behind her, and on the sidewalk hushed voices were chatting, and the street was quiet. We could see to our left across the train tracks, the huge finely wrought high stone structure that was the capital building of Kentucky before they built a new one; and we could feel how tall it was and solid, as if it had planned to be a capital forever.

"It's a wine tasting," Martha said to us smiling brightly. She holds her glass high in front of her.

A man walked right up wearing a stocking cap and a quilted jacket. He was maybe in his late twenties. He ignored Johnny and me.

"What is going on here?" he said to Martha. He was aggressive, smiling sharply, full of himself.

"It's a wine tasting," Martha said with her same intense goodwill to all, and she lifted her glass higher than before.

"Well, I'm a wino," the man said to Martha. "How do I do this?" He was not a wino. He was clean of that feeling. Only a little drunk. He was directing his attention to Martha. He wanted her attention, to get close to her.

"It's free. Just go in there," Martha said, full of sincerity.

"I don't want any Morgan David, or anything as good as that," the fake wino said, taking a step toward Martha, bumping my shoulder a bit, putting us out of the circle. "I just want some wine, any kind. How do I do this?" The fake wino looked back at Johnny and smiled brightly for assurance. He was half drunk, maybe more than half.

"You just lift the glass, put it to your mouth, and

drink it," Johnny said, and stared at the man, unsmiling. Johnny could look impenetrable when he was not smiling; and he did not move. We were finished with the man's aggressiveness toward Martha, and Martha was fazing out, looking over the man's shoulder; she began to shiver. It was easy to see the man's struggle: that ancient malady of confusion conditioned into him; and yet he didn't seem a bad man.

"Hey," the man said to Johnny. "Are you making fun of me?' Who do you think you are? Apologize, smart ass."

Johnny kept looking at the man. I know Johnny, and I know that he was seeing many things as he watched the man. He was a tough looking guy. He did not know what to make of Johnny. Johnny said nothing, just kept his gaze on the man. The man looked over our heads, and then walked to a group of three men and began to talk to them and look back our way.

"Go in quick. You're shivering," I said to Martha.

"Are you coming in?" Martha asked, her voice again full of goodwill. "It's a wine tasting, you know."

"Maybe another time," I said.

We incline to a 'Wine" that can't be seen; only its effect is seen. It did not matter to us that the shops were closed. We glanced in the window of the bookshop to see if we could see the cat that stayed there, but no sign of her. The train tracks were covered in snow. We went out and tried to balance on the rails that were slick with the snow, and Johnny began to joke about tight ropes and ten thousand foot canyons, and I gave him a push, and he pretended a fall and he rolled down into the snow between the tracks and I fell in beside him, and we lay there between the tracks and watched the snow fly above us.

Carmello's was on the corner in a very old building of its own. Inside the restaurant all was welcoming, warm, outdated and lovely. There were large photographs on the walls, old wooden tables and chairs and wooden booths worn smooth. The food was good, we knew. The father and mother cooked. There were specialties always. That night: eggplant, fish with baked onion and cheese, sweet potatoes, broccoli, yellow squash.

A scuffed wooden floor welcomed us in, and we sat in a booth by the window. It was an open booth with a hawk and someone's initials carved into the wood. The low backs of the booths let us enjoy the sweep of the room. An elderly couple sat at a fine, old, rickety, wooden table against the wall. The teenage daughter of the owner was playing the violin near the plaster bust of Benvenuto Cellini. I could see the owners, Carmello and his wife Jeanie, cooking at the edge of the huge, white stove. The daughter was playing something by Vivaldi; I knew because the elderly man at the table against the wall asked her, and I saw her say Vivaldi. I don't memorize names with music. It was something very tender, played softly. When Johnny and I stepped in out of the cold, her focus sharpened, and her music made us feel that sharpening and the smell of tomato sauce and sweet potatoes and the heat from the big stove. We knew the young girl and smiled at her, and she smiled above her violin as she played.

Carmello and Jeanie in full, white aprons greeted us smiling. We knew them well; we were all great friends when we came there for a meal. It was a restaurant of warmth, lit by lamps with red and gold shades, a clean place, wood that had been seasoned with years of use, and a family worn smooth by love and struggle. It was a place to let go, or to think, if you wished. There was history and inspiration, too, in the old black and white photographs that lined the walls: there was Carmello standing straight in uniform, decorated twice in the war.

We watched the daughter play the violin, and we smiled at her playing; it was sweetness she gave.

"Change," Johnny said.

"And our part in it," I replied, merely to answer.

"Yes, that challenge."

"A challenge we love."

"We part tonight."

"The young girl with the violin will be challenged."

"As everyone is challenged."

"I think we will always love what we do," I said.

"Yes, tonight in this warm place."

"We will make something good of it because we are here."

"It is who we are."

"It is always that way, isn't it?"

"Yes."

"Yes, we work for it."

"We will write letters spinning tales, inward tales, a language of love to sift through," Johnny said.

"Yes, letters in a different language," I said. "What we are doing inside."

"Don't have time to take a fast train," Johnny sang, catching the notes of the song, and laughing.

There were bells on the door, and they jingled, and the cold air rushed in when the door was opened. It was the man from the street, the man who called himself a wino to get close to Martha. And now he did look borderline wino, just drunk enough that his eyes had begun to glaze over. There were two men with him, all in their late twenties. I could see his anguish; he was unsettled, as if he had unfinished business with us and he had no idea what that business was. He sat at a table against the wall opposite us and kept glancing our way.

Johnny was watching the snow out the window. I think of him in my arms last night, and in his arms entwined, complete, in one sense again changed within. The snow had just begun, but we felt no cold from it, no threat of winter. It was our last night in the cabin. We needed in unexplored places. We needed to work in those regions that act as a barrier against the spirit, to go there until the job was done, until the dross was transformed and cleared, until, a little at a time, that unquenchable spirit, sometimes called doubtful, arcane or magnificent, had moved deeper. I said to him: Write me a letter, and I will write you. Say anything, and I will break the code. There can never be a parting, I told him. How much I love him; he offers me everything. We bring to each other the food of paradise because we have gone out to find it. And we go out again and again to refine it.

The man who called himself a wino ordered, and then he walked to our table. He was strong but not tall, solidly built. He still wore a sock hat. His skin was smooth and somewhat tan as if he had recently spent time out of doors. He had a scar on the back of his hand near his thumb. There was a hint of a smile when he approached, but it went away.

"Hey," he said with bluster. And being a bit drunker made him braver than before. He spoke directly to Johnny. "I was just having some fun. Don't tell me how to drink wine. I want an apology."

"Forgive me if I seemed rude," Johnny said. He spoke quietly, easy, matter-of-fact.

"Right. You don't mean it. You're a smart ass. You aren't that girl's protector."

"I mean it," Johnny said. He was unruffled, looking straight at the man, waiting to see what he would do next. Here it was, all the sadness and struggle of the world calling out for help.

The man said, "Who are you all, anyway? You act like you are something special."

"Nothing special," Johnny said.

"Maybe she is something special." He looked at me. "But you…." He looked at Johnny. "You are just a smart ass." He pulled his sock hat from his head and held it in his hands in front of him. He looked at the hat in his hands, and, as if he had exposed too much, he put the hat quickly back on his head. He needed us; something in him knew it. And of course, Johnny is not afraid of anyone—careful, but not afraid.

It was then that the woman, Julia, stood up. I did not know her. Johnny knew her. She had been listening from the booth behind us. Johnny had his back to her. I noticed her when she came in. She was tall and strong, trim and lovely, searching about, energy to burn, round silver circles for earrings, jeans, a short green jacket unbuttoned, a red sweater with sparkles and Rumi's name on it. She was taller than the man standing at our table. She swung gracefully from her booth and faced the man. "Leave them alone, Mike."

"Shove it, Julia," the man said.

"Watch your language. These people aren't like you."

"Leave me alone, Julia." He did not look at her, and his face flushed red. He seemed wary of her, a bit afraid.

"You leave them alone," she said, then she looked at Johnny, nodded to him and smiled with kindness. "How's it going, Farm Boy?"

Johnny burst into a warm smile, surprised and

happy to see Julia, maybe happy to see her alive. And I think she must have felt he was right there with her again looking for her truck on the back roads. "Julia, it's you," Johnny said. "I have wondered when we would meet again."

"Why wonder? I was out there?"

He noticed her sweater and remembered. "Nice sweater," he said. He remembered when they met she had worn that same sweater of sparkles with I'm In Love With Rumi written across it in flowing script, and that she had said she bought it in a thrift shop and that she did not know the man.

"Poet," Julia said.

"I thought you didn't know the man," Johnny said playfully.

"Thinker," she said, smiling. "I still don't know the man well. We have met briefly since you and I talked; his poems, you know. He is deep in there, isn't he?"

Johnny laughed. "Not too far away. "

Very close, I thought; not far away at all.

Johnny was especially happy to see Julia. And I liked her bright disregard, how she kept her sharpness.

"Hey, Julia, do you know these people?" Mike asked. "You know this dumb ass?"

"Last time, Mike. You shut up and leave them alone, or I'll be outside waiting for you."

From Mike's desperate look, it seemed that Julia must have come up against him in some way and won out. He became quiet and stared off into the bright kitchen.

"Olivia," Johnny said, "this is Julia, the woman I told you about. Remember? Julia and I were riding around together about a year ago on a snowy night like this one looking for her truck her boyfriend had taken."

"I've wanted to meet you," I told her. "Johnny spoke

highly of you." How could I forget her as Johnny had spoken at length of her strength and intelligence and beauty, and the possibility of self-destruction?

Julia's eyes looked down under half closed lids, thoughtful. Then she shook my hand, and a smile came, broad and confident.

She laughed and said, "I wasn't trying to pick him up."

"Well, that's not my business," I said, returning her laughter. I liked her immediately; I saw her reaching for that recondite sense of what is to be avoided and what is to be taken on.

Johnny was looking at Mike who was standing there, his head tilted away, glued to the spot. "Mike," he said, reaching to shake Mike's hand. "I'm Johnny."

He acted as if nothing had gone before with Mike; nothing fake from Johnny, just accepting Mike as he was, as he had been this night, liking him well enough. And knowing Johnny, he was seeing something in Mike: what he could become.

"And this is Olivia," Johnny said. "Sit down with us. Join us, Mike." We both shook hands with him. He shook hands like a robot, hesitant, and with a bleak look of concern, he sat next to me. Johnny gestured to Julia, and she sat beside him.

We were quiet, still and quiet. Only Johnny and I were at ease. I felt I had a new friend in Julia, someone whose intentions were like my own. I could see it in her. I could see it in the way she pushed Johnny's water glass closer to him; I could see it in the way she waited, in the way she began to settle down, patient for the unfolding, adjusting toward ease. I knew it in what cannot be said.

Johnny turned to me. "How long do we have

before we leave for the airport?"

"Maybe forty minutes," I said.

We had been looking out the glass of the big window at the snow falling. The wind was blowing the big flakes, slanting and lifting them, and we could see the life-size doll of a woman, dead of eye, static, staring blankly, sitting in a chair in the museum window on the other side of the street. Yet the snow made her better; it gave her white fur and ribbons and let her dance against the window.

Both of us, I know, were thinking we should leave now; it was thirty miles to the airport. But neither of us moved to leave. Our flights were important; if we did not catch them, the very rhythms of our lives would be changed. We knew we might never have another chance to get to the places we needed to be; we would merely get old and die. Another ticket tomorrow? What is that?

I thought of our life together, Johnny and I. I thought of walking together in the snow along where the train used to come roaring down the tunnel of trees, and holding each other by the pool of water down under the bridge. I thought of Johnny's horse, Spirit, and how we would ride double, sliding on bareback, and in the moonlight out to the back field where the fence ran along the tracks and we would put our blanket down and Spirit would stand over us and watch over the fields, and her eyes would close when she was easy, and one of her back legs would relax at the hip, and she would relax against the other three. She was a presence like the moon or the north star, our protector, Spirit, so tall against the sky when Johnny kissed me and I would kiss him. Spirit seemed to touch the Milky Way to carry on to the farthest galaxies forever. Yet when we kissed, we did not look at her. We forgot about her because we didn't need to remember her, because we were in the place that brought it all together, not because of the kiss, but because of who we were within the kiss. Whatever that love is, we had it near and we cared for it. And the white horse, Spirit, watched over us. And our love was like music that left within us romance and the imperishable, and we carried all of that with us riding home, and it stayed with us through the night and into the next day and the next. Over time, it fills us up, and the white horse Spirit is always with us. Johnny is kind; he is kind to me; he shows me he loves me; I show him; he is kind to everyone, even when he must show toughness or distance; even when that is the only avenue, his kindness is hidden there.

"Who do you people think you are, anyway?" Mike blurted. "Maybe you are just too cool. I mean, you don't seem to care about anything."

"Shut up, Mike," Julia said.

"I don't have to shut up for you. Just because you beat me once when I wouldn't hit a woman, wouldn't hit you, you can't threaten me now."

"You didn't have good aim, now did you; you were drunk, and you were bullying someone."

"You kicked me in the jaw when I wasn't looking."

"You were looking. You turned on me. You were drunk."

"I was pushing you out of the way."

"Some push."

"And the little bastard deserved it. Drop it. I don't want to get into it with you."

"Listen, Mike, can't you see these people want to eat in peace."

"Who are these people? This guy thinks he's tough."

Johnny turned in his seat to look directly at Mike. "Julia is my friend," he said. "Someone took her truck, and I helped her find it."

"That would have been Rick," Mike said.

"I'm finished with Rick," Julia said. "I've done a lot in a year." She looked at Johnny as if to say, you gave me wonder, and I want you to know I did good things in the year gone by.

"Sure," Mike said. "I heard about you and Rick splitting up. You won't do better."

"Julia and I are family," Johnny said to Mike carefully and clearly. "She is family now. I will protect her."

"You people are nuts," Mike said. "Are you threatening me?"

"I don't need protection," Julia said, and her eyes slowly narrowed.

"Yeah," Mike said. "She thinks she's kung fu."

"I'm not threatening you, Mike," Johnny said quietly.

I looked at Julia. Tears had come to her eyes. Her head was tilted forward, and her beautiful eyes were filling with tears. I knew then that she had never in her life heard the words "I will protect you." She had never felt such love coming from someone who owed her nothing, or from anyone. It was from someone who had touched her, and she did not know if he understood what he had given. From someone she imagined had forgotten her, she heard, "I will protect you." For her it was prayer, and a silent sob lifted in her chest to be loved so, and she quickly wiped the tears with her napkin. Mike saw her begin to cry and stared down at his hands, visibly unsettled. Johnny saw, too, said nothing, and waited.

"Who are you people?" Mike asked. There was frustration in his voice as if there was something urgent and vital he might lose, and he had no idea what it was.

"He lives out in Jett on a farm," Julia said, recovering her edge, her aplomb, and her smile. "He is a farmer. I don't know. Do I want to know?" She laughed freely as if all of that was secondary, under the bridge. "I give up. Who are you anyway, Johnny? Who are you, Olivia?"

Julia turned to me. She wanted to hear me talk, and just for her I started talking.

"Johnny and I met when we were seven, and fell in love, too. After that, it was just rhythms through many years. Sometimes we went hand-in-hand; sometimes we went separately. Suddenly, learning about the inner self became a discipline, a challenge. We wanted to strengthen ourselves, look behind every door. This thought came to us, and little by little, never left. Johnny had his job on the farm. I worked in the flower shop. Nothing mattered to us but learning, learning of all kinds, the mystery that we felt in life, of the self; we realized there was so much to learn, peace to fathom. We felt the fragmented shifting of our thoughts and looked there. Forgive me if I say the mystery of the self. Could it not be one of the most practical things we seek?"

Jeanie put silverware on the table before us while I was talking. She heard my last words about the mystery of the self and smiled at me. Mike began to fidget with his knife and fork.

"How about it, Johnny? Is that enough?" I asked.

Johnny laughed. "Sure. Plenty."

"You tell us something, Farm Boy," Julia said. "Have you learned to drive since we were together? Repaired any dents?" All of us laughed, but Mike. I knew the story from Johnny of the night he had driven Julia around to find her truck, and that she berated him for not following her directions quickly enough, and for the battered state of his car. And yet she said it all in the freedom she felt to be sharp with him, all in the leeway, the recognition that came naturally between them to play. When Johnny told me the story, he said that Julia's focus was impeccable, that she was close to us in what she was striving for, and that she had no clue of what that was. He told me how very much he liked her.

"I fell in love with Olivia at seven," Johnny said. "Before I was seven, I saw Olivia in the flowers and trees and the colors in the sky." He smiled.

"You have never told me that," I said, just to play.

Johnny smiled warmly. "I still see you there," he said. I could feel the devotion, always fresh between us.

"Mike," Johnny said, looking at him closely, "I grew up in this town as I imagine you did." Mike nodded, then looked again at his hands. "I stayed pretty close to the farm because I was needed," Johnny said. "When I was a young boy, I didn't know how to get around in town. I didn't know that blocks were square. After one left turn, I got lost trick-or-treating on Halloween. A kind lady helped me get back to my grandmother's house on Murray Street, or I'd still be out there."

Mike stared at his hands. "She was one of the many who helped me get along growing up," Johnny said. "I was a farm boy. I grew up with sports. I liked to ride. We had horses on the farm, but nothing fancy, just the pleasure of riding out bareback with friends. I liked stories of adventure, and I liked learning how to do things, and I didn't mind thoughts that I could not quite puzzle out. My mother and father started me out by telling me their own stories, what had touched them. They read to me, too. I went to Frankfort High School. Did you?"

Mike nodded.

"Olivia says it all," Johnny continued. "She mentions the mystery of the self. What is that? Well, I guess a mystery is just what we don't know that is possible to know; sometimes it is about the self and what can be done there. Always sounds strange to say it. Same old words people will argue about. You could say it any way you want to say it, Mike."

"Bypass me," Mike said. "So you are friends with Julia. Good luck with that. Three against one; I am the man out, and you owe me an apology." He didn't look at Johnny.

"Actually, I don't owe you anything," Johnny said quietly, looking at Mike who was looking at his knife and fork. Mike pushed them sharply away, and they slid on the Formica top toward Julia, and she stopped them deftly with her hand. He jumped up and stood by the booth and stared at Johnny, his fists clenched at his sides.

"Sit down, Mike," Johnny said quietly.

"You are drunk, Mike," Julia said. "Get out."

"No, that's okay," I said. "Stay with us, Mike. They are bringing your food to our table. I don't think you're drunk. Sit down with us and eat."

Mike looked at everyone, his eyes just shifted over us, and he sat.

"You have to catch a plane tonight?" Julia asked me. She ignored Mike.

"Yes," I said.

"Where are you going?" she asked.

"Johnny and I are going to similar places in separate planes," I told her. "Travels we wish to make."

"What kind of crazy people are you?" Mike asked. He was belligerent, but not so much as before. "You insult people, then insult them again pretending you are something mysterious. You think you're special. Well, you're not special."

"You're right, Mike," Johnny said. "We aren't special. We are doing what anyone could do, going where you could go. But our travels are not really any of your business at the moment; you have your own things to do."

"Don't say that I am right," Mike said. "You don't mean it. You don't think I'm right. Tell me what is going on with you people. Stop playing tricks."

"Change, Mike," I said. "What to do with it."

He softened because I was a woman, and he felt I had not directly insulted him. He waited. He was almost sober.

"Ask Julia," I told Mike. "She does not really know us other than an evening with Johnny. Maybe she can tell you something."

Mike would not look at Julia.

"Julia dated Rick," Mike said. "Once dropped out of school for him. She must be ignorant."

Julia's eyes narrowed. "Yeah, Mike. Ignorant. But not forever."

"Let Julia tell you," I said. "Let her tell you about us." I inclined to her, to Julia's great force, her keen attention. I knew she was not afraid. I knew she would say something. I had no idea what it would be, and I did not really care. It was up to her.

Julia sat tall, upright, flexible in feeling, and looked directly at Mike for moments before she spoke, as if she were appraising him again.

"Mike, you are an idiot. These people are not. You think you are always right. You think that you know a lot and that you have no need to change. These people do not think that about themselves. When I spent the evening driving around with Johnny in his wreck of a car, I was looking out for my own problem, but in between I was watching him. I knew something made him unlike anyone I had known, so I watched him; I felt him and listened. He didn't have to say much. I saw that he was content, and that makes me cry even now, and I saw that he was helping me, giving his time, caring about that help, without a thought that there was anything in it for him. Even in his silence he asked for nothing in return. I didn't know how to talk to him. It was a beautiful night with all the snow and the light in the sky and the green cedars shifting, but I would not acknowledge that beauty. Johnny didn't care that I had come to the point of tremendous anger inside me, my own, and that my anger was turned toward Rick. Johnny did not care to correct me, knew it would not work, so he was all love just driving me where I needed to go. I could say anything and he remained love." Julia began to cry. She put both hands to her face and cried, and she wiped the tears away and looked at me as she held back her tears, and she brushed a hand over her eyes again.

I watched Mike's eyes close until they crinkled on the sides. He jerked his head around to look out into the kitchen where the lights were bright and people were moving about. Johnny put his hand on Julia's forearm and then lifted it away.

"If we don't meet again," Johnny spoke almost in a whisper, leaning to Julia, "don't worry."

Mike suddenly stood as if to leave, hesitated with his back to the table, and then he sat back down. No one said a word. His hands moved on the table then went to the pockets of his coat and then back to the table. He picked up a spoon and turned it over and over in his fingers and watched it.

No one spoke. Our food came. The daughter still played the violin softly, improvisation, a journey she was taking as she watched us. She turned and stood at an odd angle so that when she looked out over the violin she could see our table. Only the elderly couple was still in the room. I could tell that the daughter wished to be sitting with us and wished she could enter in with all that we were saying; I know that because I know her. Some day, because of what she really wants, she will find herself hearing these things.

Mike turned the spoon over and over, and he looked to the lights of the kitchen and back to the spoon. He had heard what he had never heard before, something like the calling of a distant bell or a single cricket that sings. And what he was began to shatter.

Johnny and I had planned to have this last dinner alone to talk together, and to try not to wonder if we would live or die, if we would see each other again. We had been apart before, but this was different; we were giving ourselves to a new journey, again and again. Write me a letter, Johnny, and I will write one to you.

"Airport," Julia said. "When do you have to leave?"

"We should leave now," I said.

I noticed Mike. He started to speak. He dropped the spoon against the table. Then he said, "Wait a minute. You can't leave in this weather." He jumped up to look out the window at the snow. "What car do you drive?" he demanded.

We all looked at Mike. He looked worried; his brow was furrowed.

"Johnny's car," I said.

"I'll drive you in my car," Mike said. "It goes anywhere: four wheel drive, mud tires. When the salt trucks can't go, I am out there. You shouldn't try it."

"You've been drinking, Mike," Julia said quietly.

"Hell, Julia, I'm sober." I think Mike was dead sober.

"Maybe," Julia said. The pressure to meet the planes was in all of us.

"Okay, Queen of Sheba," Mike said with intense concern for us in his voice. "You drive my car." Then he looked at Julia as a brother might, with trust in her for that moment. His voice settled for the first time: "We'll all go, Julia. These people can't drive out in this."

"Okay, I'll drive your car," Julia said. She looked to us. "What do you think?"

Both Johnny and I knew his old red Lincoln to be a good snow car; that it would make the trip. Both of us drove well in any weather. We had planned to be alone before we parted, and yet we each knew what to do without asking the other.

"Fine with me," I said. "Thank you."

"Sure," Johnny said. "Thanks. That would be a great help. Let's go."

We went to the kitchen door to tell the owners of the restaurant goodbye in all the bright, hot kitchen light. It was like home. In those moments, I knew what it was to be in a kitchen like that one, and cook, to be in that bustle to cut onions, wash lettuce, shake the skillet, turn the flapjacks. Johnny and I could cook. We learned it in the country from our mothers. Maybe another time; tonight I had to go.

We said goodbye to the daughter with the violin. We knew we were going to miss her and her music, and we told her so, and she played us out the door, and the bells jingled that were hanging on the doorknob, and the romantic touch of her music followed us into the street and changed the street into something more, her music lifting free from her violin, improvised, mingling about like a butterfly in the driving snow.

We were thirty miles away, and we hoped the planes would fly.

Johnny and I sat together in the backseat. It was nice and dark back there. Outside, the snow was falling slowly, flakes floating down and flashing by like little stars in the lights. The car was a huge, very old Chrysler that Mike had modified and souped up, made fast and comfortable and clean; and the seats were of a thick, soft, saffron wool, and the engine and the mufflers made the heavy, bass, humming sound of a plane cruising at night. Mike sat up front with Julia, and I felt his sudden faith in her when he handed her the keys, the way he sat back and let her drive. Johnny and I felt private and far away in the backseat. We scooched down a bit in the seat and put our heads together. We felt safe. We were brave about parting, but how could we be completely brave, our heads softly together, holding hands for maybe a last time?

Julia was pushing the big car hard in the storm, speeding on the snow-blanketed roads. There were no other cars; no one was out there. We came into the airport turn in a long, slow, graceful slide, yet we all felt safe. Forcing it in the long driveway to the terminal, Julia hit the curves shifting down and sliding. At the curb, we jumped out and ran. Mike ran with us, and the satchels we were carrying seemed light, and as we ran we would slide purposefully to hold our balance in the running, and the air was cold and the snow fresh and light on the ground.

Mike took my satchel from my hand and carried it.

Julia parked the car in a towing zone and ran with us. I ran next to Johnny. When he would slide in the snow, he would smile at me, and then he would take my hand and we would run and slide together and laugh. The airport lights made the snow sparkle, and snow got into the tops of my shoes from sliding, and I could feel the coolness it brought. I could feel Johnny at my side running and our warm hands when we held them to pull each other along. What an amazing time, I thought; what miracles of love that are always coming: to run—the four of us together—the four of us running.

Out by the gate, parked nose to nose, both planes were warming up, and as we ran through the small, empty terminal, the man at the counter quickly raised his hand high and pointed us toward the gate, and we ran and pushed the glass doors open and burst out together into the night again. There was only a wire fence with a wire gate. The snow was floating, big flakes floating down cold against our faces. Mike walked up to Johnny and held out his hand. "Thank you," Mike said. He kept his hand in Johnny's, and searched in Johnny's eyes. "Thank you, too," Johnny said. "Let's meet again. It would be good to meet again."

"Yes, let's meet again," Mike said quietly. And he turned from Johnny, and he came to me and shook my hand and smiled self-consciously; then suddenly he put his hand gently on my shoulder, and then he moved away.

Julia was crying when she put her arms around Johnny. She was tall, and one of her arms was around his neck and the other around his shoulder, and she was crying and she could not talk and she held him tightly, sobbing quietly against him. Then she turned away without looking into Johnny's eyes, and she came to me and she hugged me and she was still crying, and she held me until she could let go; and she turned away, and she and Mike walked quickly into the terminal, and I saw them stop by the bay window to watch us go.

We held each other, Johnny and I. There can be no more unsettling moment in the romance that spreads its gift over the earth than when those in love must part into the unknown. And yet, we can be brave.

Our planes took off at the same moment on parallel runways in opposite directions. If you were watching them from the ground the planes would make an open V in the air, the two sides perfectly balanced, rising to the distance as if in slow motion, as if in mathematical perfection: a triangle missing its last line; or to some, a heartbreak to see a loved one lift away through the snow.

Now I choose to speak a different language, to see the two planes side by side, balanced as if to make a point on the concrete runway. When the planes lift off into the sky in opposite directions making two sides of a perfect triangle, and snow is falling, too, and rain, and rivers and buildings collapse, children sleep, mandrakes moan, clocks are chiming, where is the last line?

The last line rides on what Johnny and I have done to coalesce the force that we have made welcome. It has condensed within us because we made room for it in the fields where the ego slakes its clutter. As we clear brush from those fields, the great beauty begins to land from where it has been circling forever.

And so, from plane to plane between us the last line comes; it is always out there dancing. The last line is as palpable as a comet skimming through space. And in that we have the lineage passed on from person to person, from age to age. It becomes safe within us. We are a full part of each other and of the universe itself as that force completes. Planes must fly in different directions, breaking the hearts of lovers everywhere, though we accept no devastation. In tenderness, Johnny and I, violets now in springtime; we are brave.

Down on the ground, behind the bay window, through filters of their own making, Julia and Mike look toward the sky at the silver planes lifting off like daggers through the snow. They look toward the sky because they touch—without thinking of its existence—the light that is always in tow; the light as tendrils filters into Julia and Mike on pathways they are trying to clear: earth moving, road building, meditation, service, patience, breathing, brush fire; there is work to do to bring beauty to the cells. Julia and Mike recognize us; we recognize them. A man or woman does not have to be insane to be sensitive to what cannot be seen.

Julia, Mike, Johnny and I had something inside of us that enabled recognition: to each what was given, to each what was earned. Mike held himself close, Julia came on like magnetism and fire. Something was operating in each at a certain pitch. The recognition is simply there, like a pool of light touched, then glowing.

The triangle is completed across the sky between two planes rising. For now, I build this triangle with words because I choose to build it; I choose for a moment to speak a different language. The triangle is standing on one of its points there on the airport runway; and yet, as I move away from that point, over time, back off from its up and its down, there will be no up and down for me in the universe. The triangle swiftly spinning marks as symbol the absence of space and time; or let it mark action as the essence of this journey on earth. I will always be with

Johnny because of the last line filling the space. It is our warmth that whispers separateness: don't go, don't leave; it is our arms holding each other tightly then, maybe for the last time. I feel in Johnny the whisper of heartbreak, and wish I could lift that whisper from him. I feel my own, and wish there was another way, yet change gives no quarter.

I know that Julia and Mike saw the planes rise as planes, not as symbols; and they could not take themselves away from watching them go. They engage more closely tonight than ever before, the inexpressible field that among us glows. Julia and Mike whisper peace; they whisper love as the planes keep lifting. Each hopes someday to be on such planes as that, and to know the last line that is not a line, as if a comet that is not a comet skims as truth to them through space unseen. We all long for violets in springtime.

Johnny's Letter

Dear Olivia,

I am alive in the mountains in a foreign world. Somewhere deep you will know where I am. A man I have begun to know will send this letter for me. He is familiar, a traveler in his own land. I know he will do his best to send this letter on its way, because we ate together before an open fire and laughed. You have always said that I could tell the good from the bad.

In this inviolate air some things die away. I have no old friend around me. My cameraman, Jake the note taker, is dead. A bullet, under a cypress tree in the moonlight, killed him three days ago. We took cover around him and all was quiet. We buried him in a shallow grave and moved on. I made camp here with them. What else am I to do but try to make my way home? I won't talk about Jake. What does it mean to lose a part of me that built up over all the years?

What a friend you have been to me. When we were together, so briefly in the beginning, so off and on it now seems, I loved you with all I could love, my deep affection, all the possessions I am holding, and all the beauty I had ever mustered in my heart, belong to you.

When I left home I shouldered longing and doubt. Yet something has died in me, something that needed to die, a welcome death, three days ago. I will no longer make worlds that tire me. Tonight I do not worry. How could that be? I could take fire in the next moments, but only if there is a part of me that still needs to die.

The evening Jake was killed I found a way to rest.

Night came and we built a small fire to cook the shank meat of a mountain goat we had bagged at the edge of the canyon. Fine horns led the goat across the plain, sparks flew from animal hooves and animal eyes as he bolted. Sunset blazed with a purple haze.

There was a soldier with us, a high officer, so it seemed by his bearing, older, involved in reconnaissance. I was in transition when we met up, looking for a road home. He moves selflessly in these mountains; he works to save lives. When he began to talk, I forgot there was a war or that we were soldiers. It was a midnight that suddenly became vast and clear; I was careless of tomorrow. It was the insurgent breeze that touched me with feminine hands.

A woman came out of the darkness, leaned and whispered in the man's ear. Then she smiled gently to me as if there were some lasting intimacy between us, and she took the long bladed knife from my hand on which I had held the dripping goat meat above the fire. She knew that my muscle and my mind were cramping; she must have known, for without a word she relieved me of that burden. She saw truly the opening to help me and moved in to help. She was dark-eyed with a stunning grace, dressed in tight mountain clothes. It was not cold and her shoes were light like moccasins, wolf skin with sky blue tassels and beads. It seemed to me that she had whispered help and encouragement into the man's ear, with no words at all.

The reconnaissance man unveils the forces that surrounds us, forces I will know in countless forms. He is the man whose worlds I gather: in time I have understood the mundane, Olivia—the world of everyday chores and aberrant thought; I understand men, children, women, firelight. I am clear about all of that which men call art. I understand artists: the writers, the painters, the singers and their songs; I understand a man who might work in iron in his backyard making a lattice of morning glories reaching to the sky. There is nothing I don't understand as I write to you from this all-embracing vein of air. People speak of mountain air, but what do they experience within? Words are a common lot.

You say your friend as been asked to marry, and so have we all in the rhythm of choices. I will respond now as if it is you who has been asked to marry; and yet, I will be talking to your friend. You and I know that we were married many years ago, and in this realm of my letter, as in the realm of the invisible, there exist no rules of sequence or rote. Yet, let me speak tonight; I feel like writing to you, feeling your warmth, leaning on you in my story here of what together we know. Tell me if I say it right.

It is not whom you will marry, but what portion of the universe, what layers of the universe you will marry, the strata that make him. I do not have confidence in the man who has asked you to marry. I will not use his name, as his name brings tension with the sound. You know him as I do. He was born for struggles not near to your own, and he has misused his time. He is not up to what you can do. He has forged veils of unknowing, which he decorates with charm. I know why you tell me of his request. You tell me, because you know that I know him too, when he trudges in with all the conventions of the culture pasted on him, and words of love for you. At his worst he is at his best. No amount of tenderness will change him. One must grow in stature to see his backward pull upon the soul.

Yes Olivia, there are no drugs or alcohol here; it would be witless to imagine them here. They would damage the landscape. It is only the remiss who go to chemicals and stay with them, even in the parched valley. If one does not use those false cavaliers of the nervous system, still he may drink the smoke of false ideas to slake an acquisitive thirst. He will drink hardened opinion, hope without truth, habits of emotion that live in the vat with the drugs. He is then merely a puritan without a working brain. Why court laughter with wine in hand? Why court love with ritual thought? Why shift about on a thin plane, a flat plane with unlovely décor, careless of the brain; never in this world, around this fire, over here. In that man's world, there is nothing deep-seated in his laughter. Don't trust him. He is like so many others. To give us strength, we may call in from beyond the liquid sun, always freshly falling through space; and in the dusk when the sun is playing with the clouds, we may skip a rock over a pool of rainwater in the low meadow where the tiny green frogs sing flashes of mystical sound into the air, sing high-pitched change into the heart. The rock you lean low to sail across the water is rain in the hand, the stone of stones.

Around this campfire mystery comes in on the warm wind, and her smile is there, so that she can take for a while our burden, and leave us changed. She visits and goes away, and each time, leaves a part of her, until we are cherished within time forever. She is enduring. She merely loves. She lifts all fears for she is impervious to fear. She is engaged with all things just as they are, Olivia. There is not much to see around a campfire in these strange, high, sage-strewn mountains; the answers are silently conveyed. This generous night implores us to understand what we are doing and how we might wish to carry on.

This man, this high officer, gathering intelligence as I write, leans comfortably against a stone. Firelight bathes our faces. He just said this:

"Why do people care so much about what is not worthy of their care?"

Olivia, I love you, of course, and I want you to have what will lift you up forever, and the man who requests your hand is not the answer. He is of that ancient glue that makes a woman sluggish.

The man at the campfire just spoke quietly. His message is sent, yet only understood with time and effort. He said that every thought has a parallel action. He said that when the intelligence of the heart permeates, its answer is the moment, imbued with all that is sweet. He said that thought and action become one then, arriving simultaneously from the same source.

This woman, who is now lying on her side, leaning on one arm, her head cradled in her willing hand, seems to be, if you saw her, merely a woman waiting for the time to pass. Yet, I know more of that. I know she is waiting for nothing. Olivia! It is an inner state that moves us all. The design of this campfire spreads evenly throughout our being. A wolf howls. It is not Jack London's wolf full of raw emotion. The wolf sings differently to us; he sings of eternity, though still we know he longs for meat.

If I were a soldier I would protect you until the end of time, and since I would protect you until the end of time, I am a soldier.

Why give our wondrous life to people who lash their brain with chain to a muddled world? They believe that others operate in no higher strata than their own.

How can limits work when they don't exist? There are rungs in the ladder out to freedom.

I may be dead tomorrow, and this letter may not reach you. Yet I write with confidence, as you are the only one I know who could share this blazing campfire. You break through softly tonight as through the shimmer of a bubble you and I made in play, you just break into this soft mountain night with the help of that airborne spin of energy and power, as when a child might travel in dream.

The man just stood and stretched and tossed a branch on to the fire, laughed and spoke of the moment, and how we shape it perpetually without even knowing it is there. He can say those things for he knows I hear him. If I am here where the moment reigns made of something everywhere that could press until one receives and feels nothing, I must be able to listen.

Build a campfire with us, Olivia. Why consort with the watchmakers? They work with digits and tiny wheels. The wheels warp; the digits skew; the watch runs down; where is the power of eternity? We have always known what I mean.

The stars twinkle here and slide across the sky like the voice of a whippoorwill. The fire jumps and sparkles. Her eyes flash as she takes in the beauties of our camp, their light skims across the space between us, and what is hers is mine; our electric seeing cuts across the darkness, the embrace of her smile is my own.

If you would marry such a man, Olivia, will his darkened energy in intimacy burden your soul? Will his focus on irrelevancies become the close, charismatic thief of your time? Will his worries burden you? And he will worry, and he will lift his worries up like idols on a pedestal, and he will demand they be acknowledged. That's what people do. They are good at it. They worry and decline; there is no question. It is the easy way. I can see it in the choppy eyes of wolves staring in from the blackness. Those eyes mean nothing around this campfire. There is a ring of protection against the snarling wolves.

There has never been anything like this night. It is night with gentle love. True there are only mountains and sky, stars and wind and the moon. Even the eyes of the wolf that howled have gone. The red firelight is all over us. We have no worries. There is the threat of death by killers on every side, something like the threat of chemicals, human traffic, sleepwalkers and drunks, bad food and opinion. We face those threats, yet without worries, only things to do. The splendid mystery of this night's tenderness is what we have chosen over time.

"Do not marry that man", is a call to pray. Run quickly from all people like him, man or woman. Quickly, behind the lamppost! Be at ease as they pass on by arguing the nonsense of their times. The lamppost is tall and burns with the lamp oil of the ocean that falls from the sky, and its rays spread over you in the street, out of a ray gun from beyond the farthest planets, a playful, sleek ray gun from a space movie, streamlined, a ray gun gone to peace, where the little green, grimacing space invaders are winking out! Play, Olivia! Have fun! Run quickly, jump into the doorway, while the rain rains gently in, misting. And all like him will double step on by and disappear in traffic looking for the matrix of Tweedledum and Tweedledee. You stand in the doorway in your sea green dress, and all the street is singing its love song in an octave so advanced it can only be heard as a push within the cells. Green taxis go by and blue touring cars, and a spinning, gold-laden carousel with wild horses up upon it grazing in the moonlight, their backs to the rain, living in your life story as poetry, phantom-like, elegant, at ease.

If I die as a soldier it will not be up to me. I hope you get this letter. Maybe it will come by express on the wings of a high-flying bird, or in the wind-tossed mane of a pinto pony stretching out passionately to beat the clock; and you will hold this letter in your hand, which may be enough for you to pierce the veil of time.

The woman just moved. She stretched out, and nestled her arm behind her head. She is wearing the tropics on a scarf. On it is a red seabird, a palm tree leaning toward the sea, a man and a woman side by side at the edge of the sand focused on the humming of a shell. Here at our camp, the woman is looking at the stars with her eyes closed. Her breathing is visible to me. The firelight crosses her body in gentle waves. Her breathing seems balanced as if she were aware of her breath in some way, until she let her breath go to move on its own, rising and falling. She is a bed of leaves or a pillow for my head to rest on. If I think it, I am there breathing. You are near tonight, Olivia.

When you are here I would that I could love you. I mean to hold you tenderly, your lips against mine, your patience and full acceptance in surrender, nothing but starlight in your pockets. And why should we tap our foot to songs of sweet sorrow? Stay away from the masquerade. Step aside. You catch a plane here. I meet you in the air.

Is there more to light than people know? Morning will be here soon. The dawn is ours when it is magenta like a sprightly pomegranate, and green like the pale glass green leaves of springtime. In the old poetry a pomegranate would refer to love. And springtime! With the deer rushing up the hill in the dusk, perfectly quiet as they sail and lift in rhythm with the spinning of the planet. Olivia, we know springtime can bring all the ripple and touch of new singing from the trees, while the baby rabbits run in curves, hopping over a twig as if the twig were a little river, and the two of us walk out barefoot in the fine coolness of the new grass, and in the high field the green shoots flame, so that sun-drenched, when daylight fades, we press closely each to each—all of it light-soaked, breathtaking.

We came together; we then went away. This night is too pure to think of comings and goings like those. We are already swept up in each other's arms. Nearby bullets fly; death wrenches free to wander aimlessly. Here death has no more power than hometown blood on a windshield, no more power than the terrible static that disturbs minds, no more than the death of the nervous system from doses of sloe gin, blood red and bitter sweet —no more power in death here than in a broken heart.

Bake me cookies, Olivia, and I will bake cookies for you. Send them to me in care of the mountains and the harvest moon. I am happy with what you make. Are you happy too? Isn't it a state of mind, a mood for the force of the cosmos to sup with, like cookies and milk left on the hearth for a saint in a new birth time of spirit? The cookies are gone in the morning, and yet, left in their place are gifts resplendent, salutes from the wise. Something magnificent happens, again and again.

This is no joke, Olivia. What does it mean to be in love? There is only so much time to use for traveling to a place like this.

The man of whom I speak is stretched out, leaning against the smooth, arabesques of wood I carried up to feed the fire. He spoke again of nowhere to go, nowhere to advance but inward, while keeping the world around us in order and in its place. Give the world its due, he said, while swimming deep. The man, our thinking, laughs. No words to describe this shimmering night as it settles under the skin, a night of vision, of ease and simplicity under a passionate fan of stars.

I don't need to hear them now: the words he spoke; and certainly this mountain woman with grandeur in her eyes, trim with soft hair falling to her shoulders, and rose petals blowing all around her, with white gardenias fresh and fluttering to lift and drift against her soft lips, with her moon drenched skin showing above her moccasins, and the luxury of columbine at her breasts; she doesn't need to hear them either. Olivia, do I hear your breathing?

There is a saying I remember. Didn't we find it together? It is about relaxing the mind and learning to swim. Who was it first spoke those words? Does it matter who it was who said them first? You and I have always known that it does not matter.

The woman has been writing. In one hand she holds a sheet of paper dappled with rain. I see her writing now in the firelight. She has finished writing, and she has looked up to meet my eyes briefly, as one who is finished writing looks up. She folds the paper carefully and hands it to me. In the fire's light the paper has the look of an ancient parchment. I open it now and tilt it toward the coals. Red sparks wriggle up and surround her. It is her poem. She is saying:

The night screen is so thin;
False lights are burning;
We could die here, and yet…

Is there really any doubt
For those with aching arms
In their times of rising and falling,
Still lithe and untouched?
The world of affairs is a partial thing.
The spring night hums in our ears.
Green blazes from the earth
Trust lolls against every tree
And lamppost,
Start with that false self
As it falls from favor:
That intricate structure
Haphazardly built,
Shouldered too long.
So that in time,
Moment by moment,
You will vow to change,
And I will help you.
I will offer you everything:
Wakefulness at dawn,
Ease into sleep,
Food for your table,
The honey of my arms,
Kisses fresh and often.
I will listen to your words
And give you words to soothe your mind.
I will smooth your muscles
When you have held up the gates of the day.
I will dance for you and with you
To music that awakens your sense of time.
I offer you timelessness,
Freedom from fear and hurry;
I offer myself.

There is nothing I do not offer,
Nothing I won't deliver,
And now it is up to you
To rearrange,
To relinquish,
To travel deep into the moment,
To become worthy of my many offers.
I wish you peace,
And dreams that are sweet.

The woman has closed her eyes and turned her cheek warmly against her arm. The campfire glows. Her eyes are as softly closed as the closed eyes of a little child who went to bed secure and happy. Olivia.

Olivia, do not marry anyone who could make your world difficult forever. Yet, if you will marry someone worthy, then before you say yes, ask him to pledge that he will allow your inborn freedom to give all it takes to travel to these high mountains and build ancient, tender fires like this one, even against his jealously, even if it is I who am there with you to gather the arabesques of wood forever. Bullets fly. We must give them no chance with us.

And if you marry into the world on the running tides, marry a kind man, one who is tender beyond his years. Olivia, in this inner world of change, I do not believe you will find a man of the stature who can be your equal. He will not be up to what you can do if he represents a fragmentary expression of being. He will be merely an idea that lives and dies so accept no burden from him. Blend only with truth. Marry the man who will give you all his kindness, a man who will respect your seeking. Marry a man with no taste for chemicals; a man who is free of such things, as they leave unrelenting structures in the brain; and the focus deflects from the foremost thing. Marry a man who can respect what he cannot fathom, for this man would give a woman room to experiment as a new being in a new time.

As you marry in the ardent press of change, in the gift of trial and error, marry all in life that loves you dearly. A man who was born with love in his heart, and who received love from those who helped him grow, this man will have an edge on how to love, what human love might be. Marry a man who respects your freedom to seek inwardly, even if he cannot grasp your seeking with his heart. A man with whom you will find your freedom to plumb the depth, however quietly and privately you might quest, could be a man to marry. If he is a sarcastic man, step back and think; yet, if he is a strong man who tries to see clearly what is in his path, be sure his strength is not arrogance in disguise.

Have I talked all at once of many things? We all marry, Olivia, the thoughts we bring within us; we take care with how they work, from where they come. And the intuitive, she blossoms in peace; on her delicate fingers she wears golden rings. Life on the ground, with whom do we spend it? We intend to choose wisely, to become the friend of perception.

The campfire glows; the wolf howls; the note taker is dead; the man speaks; the woman smiles. Is it our precious time, the fleeting chance, the possibility of human excellence? Protect your being. Seek long. Blend only with truth. I don't need to say it. All of this is what you are. I am listening too. We stretch ourselves across the stars.

What a beautiful life we have had, Olivia, laughing and playing, with so much peace and quiet together. Who else but you could I be writing to tonight; who else will understand but you, even if this letter never arrives?

White Gardenias,
Johnny

Olivia's Letter

Dearest Johnny,

A man just shattered my rear window with a rock. Like ice, it scatters the light. It was his tap on my shoulder for attention—his whisper to unsettle me—and now he is gone. Is he merely a thought?

A woman goes by; she sees me sitting here; I tell her my need, that my car is broken. Her body shifts from me, her eyes hold blindly along the brick wall. On the white brick is a painting of a tiger. "They are good for you," the caption says. Slices of red and green watermelon float by as Viking long ships on the prowl, the woman—a solemn figurehead with wooden hair and wooden eyes.

Are they finished with me, or will they come back? I am in my car writing with a pencil and a notebook I used in school. The car has stopped running, something off in the system. In this neighborhood people live in chaos. A dead zone. Waiting patiently to develop the situation, I am alert to do my best. This neighborhood is all neighborhoods, the people all people; it is the environment within for many.

Are you still safe in the high mountains? Thank you for the most beautiful white gardenias of your letter.

I am your Olivia. Hi Darling. In the coin of our letters, we are two forces making one. We speak in that one force of a fresh world.

I will write to you of things we know. It will strengthen me as I describe these streets of danger for those seekers coming after. Our togetherness is the final state of being in which to live, the hidden force of spirit, that amazing romance.

That force fashioned our embrace that night, cheek to cheek in the moonlight filtering through the cypress tree, through the attic window, to carry intelligence into our willing arms. It was the night we turned from the lockdown simplicity of electricity, to something more. Among the summer leaves, through the warm screen, it came, while crickets played a song of eternity.

Electricity! Double-edged in gift and damage for humankind! It has infringed, step by step. It takes tremendous discipline to use electricity, and then to break free to its origin. The false self haphazardly thrown together breaks free to nowhere. It worships status. It worships food and drink, and drugs, and fear, and facts as if they were a treasure. The outer list goes on and on. The list of inward necessity is short. When you know, worship of things ends.

Do not marry that woman, Johnny. She is of the glue that makes a man sluggish. I say this as a metaphor for other things, just as you have said it. There is no woman, no man, of whom we speak, although they are out there, they are surely out there.

Chaos in the mind comes easy. Do nothing, be lazy and you have chaos. Oppose chaos, and living begins. Such a woman is fragmented; leave her where she lies. I speak these words you know—to let another pick them up. We live like the wind, Johnny.

I am writing fast. I need to get out of here, safely. My sense is not to leave the car—for the moment.

I know what it means to love and be loved because of you. I know what it means to give.

A man walks toward my car from the street side. He wears a dark coat. The wildness in his face blazes with arrogance. His fervor flares to damage. It is the imprint of false ambition, upbringing, the history of his brain. He screams for attention.

I need to deal with this.... Hold on, Johnny.

I roll down the window. He is yelling at me. His speech is riddled with curses—cursing—the dead language, a language of anger and laziness in a modern world. He yells that he knows what to do, he screams for attention. He could hail from anywhere. I ignore him. Merely a phantom. I speak to him lovingly of Mother Nature. I tell him stories of the countryside, like this: "In the fall when the leaves on the wind-swept trees change, the colors turn gently red and gold, and that's when the long-legged cranes fly south and sing their love songs across the sky." He fades. Gone.

There is a lot of trouble in the mind, isn't there, Johnny? We know that the culture of truth starts within.

Hey Johnny, love is in the air we breathe. We have made a place for love to harbor. Yes, Johnny, the lower and the higher form of it: love leading to love.

I was taken with how you expressed it in your letter. You said, "It is not whom you will marry, but what portion of the universe, what layers of the universe you will marry."

Yes, Johnny, I know what you mean. All choices are a marriage, even the smallest choice made when no one is around. No ceremony at all, just one person making a choice. You remember the saying that gave us strength, "Merely a cup of tea, and you must answer it."

This is a chaotic street: universal; the few cars that do go by are carrying only phantoms watching the evening news. I will wait in the car for now. It is my pleasure to answer your letter; I answer what cannot be answered with what cannot be told.

Hold on Johnny! A phantom just pulled his car in front of me, got out; he could be trouble. He is carrying a suitcase.

As you said to me, I say, also, to you: "I hope you get this letter. Maybe it will come by express on the wings of a high-flying bird, or in the wind-tossed mane of a pinto pony stretching out passionately to beat the clock; and you will hold this letter in your hand, which may be enough for you to pierce the veil of time."

He walks to my window without hesitation. He opens the suitcase. It is filled with money. He is a new bit of trouble, Johnny. He thinks I am a woman he can buy for a million bucks.

"Listen fellow," I threaten. "You don't know me. I am spirit; I can only be earned. When I am earned, phantoms like you die in the process."

He is of the weakness in the strata. He fades.

I am near to the warmth of your flickering campfire, Johnny.

Your words, I hear them, the white gardenias you offer. Remember when you said: "We all marry the thoughts we bring within us; we take care with how they work, from where they come."

And then you added so clearly, so sweetly: "And the intuitive, she blossoms in peace: on her delicate fingers she wears golden rings."

How amazing when the intuitive is given "a clean, well-lighted place" within us to operate, here on these feral streets, or in the artistry of a quiet café. It is the same mysterious fuel that moves two doves, sleek and innocent and clear of eye, leaning wing-to-wing and cooing softly, or dancing away from the leopard, brutally fast, who jumps high to bight them in the air.

"Quickly, behind the lamppost." you wrote in your letter. "Be at ease as they pass on by arguing the nonsense of their times. The lamppost is tall and burns with the lamp oil of the ocean that falls from the sky, and its rays spread over you in the street."

Hey Johnny, it is a mysterious world to unravel. What does it take to do the unraveling? How forceful must we be? How beautiful the evening star, Venus perhaps, with one little bird singing to us of springtime.

Two women and two men are walking together down the sidewalk. They are talking together and smiling. They are animated and walking briskly. They look as if they are going out on the town, for dinner maybe, the women wearing bracelets and high heels. The men are in felt hats that seem from an older fashion. They have stopped on the sidewalk, a few steps from my car. The women are wearing summer dresses. They look nice; they have a bounce in their walk.

"Hello, my name is Olivia. Could you help me?" I ask. "My car has broken down."

They turn to me smiling. One of the men opens the car door for me. Both men sweep off their hats in a happy, polite gesture of warmth and greeting, kind smiles. The woman in the green dress opens the hood of my car, another holds a light, and they all four lean in to the engine to see the cause. The woman in the blue dress slides up with her belly across the car's fender and leans deep under the hood to inspect something there. One man holds the back of her legs to give her balance. The woman with the light shifts and turns. The other man holds tools that appeared as if from nowhere, and hands them in.

In no time, they step back smiling. "Good as new",

the woman with the light says.

"Start her up," the woman in the green dress, who leaned in, says. Both women are warm and cheerful. The man who held the woman's legs, opens the car door for me. "Thank you," I say. "You are welcome," he says. Our gestures are of caring and of love.

I knew the engine would start. Love always starts when people come together in generosity, when ignorance and anger do not lead.

Your letter, Johnny, speaks of the inner universe; it is in the functioning of the means. We appraise and continue to sustain the many tiers of our travel. At sunrise, in the singing of the little frogs, the crickets' hymns, and in the sound of the galaxies spinning, the secret is revealed —an internal secret protected by its demand for giving, and its immediate unlikelihood to exist.

Yes, culture will always leave home broke, and it breaks many. The ones it breaks are those who buy into their culture too deeply with the heart, because soon that culture will morph and die, and so will they. Your letter is about spirit as a palpable force, like a touch on warm arms that respond. You wrote, "It was the insurgent breeze that touched me with feminine hands." Lovely way to say something that cannot be said.

And the little frogs! "We skip a rock over a pool of rainwater in the low meadow where the tiny green frogs sing flashes of mystical sound into the air, sing high-pitched change into the heart."

I remember that evening with you, skipping rocks on the wonderfully wide and fresh pool of rainwater, a bright pond in a green field. The evening light was blue and gold. And the little frogs were singing brightly, chanting with us, setting up new pathways in our brain with transformative sound, pathways that lead to awareness and far-reaching happiness.

Those sounds cut into the moment, opening avenues within us. In truth, there is only the moment. And yet, the future leans against the moment and makes itself available to one who functions there. Yes, Johnny.

In your letter, you said: "Do not marry that man."

You bet, I won't marry that man, the strata he represents: the false of the inner world, the false of the outer world. You and I speak the language of love, a code that is not a code. We both know that "that man", might not be a man at all—but can be the input within and without—that holds a person back from traveling the road to consciousness.

And this, you write: "… green taxies go by and blue touring cars, and a spinning gold-laden carousel with wild horses up upon it grazing in the moonlight, their backs to the rain, living in your life story as poetry, phantom-like, elegant, at ease."

Ahh, you speak of inspiration, Johnny, the poetic beauty that we love and that loves us, as we look to the world of nature and dream. Truth is to love, traveling in one's own land, active, to open up pathways in the brain itself; truth, as practical as it gets.

You said that we should choose playfulness in life. You wrote: "Play, Olivia! Have fun! Run quickly, jump into the doorway while the rain rains gently in, misting."

Yes, Johnny. It is our birthright to play. When I think of you, I smile. It is a smile of tenderness. I am at play, Johnny, my love. We are two peas in the same pod, and there are not even two of us any longer!

I get out of the car, Johnny. I put on my raincoat. It is a plain raincoat. It keeps the dampness away, and it has some warmth. Now, I will take this struggle to the street. I will carry with me my discipline. I look a bit like everyone else. It is a long way out of this neighborhood. It is not a rare fix to be in; everyone faces it, whether they aspire to transform or not. We all begin in the landscape of forgetfulness.

As I survey the streets, I am thinking of that mountain goat you mentioned in your letter. That beast we know. You wrote: "Fine horns led the goat across the plain, sparks flew from animal hooves and animal eyes as he bolted." Yes, that animal lives within us all. We are born with it; the animal comes with us. When, finally, comes the call to be aware of this animal, to form reins to guide it, to become impervious to its lead. The intercept of spirit was the mountain woman who relieved you of that burden. You described her this way: "She saw truly the opening to help me and moved in to help. She was dark-eyed with a stunning grace, dressed in tight mountain clothes." Of course, Johnny, I am that woman.

Remember what I brought up for us some years ago in the Apple Green Cafe? I remember well. I said that we must laugh with the world, and laugh at its warped, unruly side to keep distance. I said that we must begin to engage the inner force of humility, or we will never know what humility is, what compassion and dispassion are, or giving, or love, or living that love.

I step out. The street is quiet. It is raining lightly, a kind, protective rain, like that first green, spring morning we walked out together into the foothills of the mountain. The street I am facing at this moment is a street of scars.

In this chivalrous rain, there is a mist across the concrete from building to building. The mist starts at my waist and moves higher. It is fresh, like walking in a beam of light that heals. I turn the corner.

Suddenly I am surrounded on all sides. I take a few steps to put my back against a cold, brick wall.

The man who did not grow to be a man, the one who screams and sends curses which rebound in self-defeat, is walking toward me with shuffling steps.

Here, too, is the man who shattered my car window. Not unlike a whisper of negative thought, he is threatening me with a heavy, jagged stone, rife with fossils. He, too, is a fossil, dry and embedded.

Walking beside the fossil is the blind hustler holding up a million-dollar bill, reaching out for me with the other hand, grasping with his claw.

That carved figurehead, that woman on the front of a marauding long ship, who earlier turned her eyes to the wall, so near to the green and red watermelons, comes shivering up to complete the prison around me. It is as if she is about to explode with fear and anger; her hands quiver.

I am surrounded in a half circle, my back against the wall. I know this enemy.

I step toward them. I know each one of them now, and all of their variations. That knowledge of their characteristics and their place in time gives me the advantage. It is the advantage anyone could have.

I step toward them consciously. They retreat from the shock, taking slow steps backward. They begin to glow; their colors brighten; and, I feel an increased pressure from their command to destroy me. I give them the power of my attention, consciously. In the beginning—remember it, Johnny? Still struggling, we gave our attention wrongly; we called them out unconsciously, and began the process of clearing. Yet, I call them out now, with purpose, to show those who will come after us, that enemy they must oppose within: anger, worry, inaction and the rest.

And finally, then, in the most stupendous move a being on earth could make in a lifetime, you withheld your attention, Johnny, to redirect it into the recondite, far-reaching process toward spirit.

I begin to breathe slowly, inhaling and exhaling, focusing my attention inward. I retreat a step at a time. Their glow begins to evanesce. Disabled, they are drawn helplessly toward each other. Rather like an opaque bubble, they encapsulate—exiled and indistinct.

I leave them be. They are now one thing to me. The disruptive is under one roof. They are there, but not my own. Love does not turn, in need, to anger, but love lives in awareness.

My attention then shifts to a deep concentration, spoken of in poetry as a rose because of the beauty there, a concentration imposed on the moment for what is true in life, what is deeply real: that incomparable state of being that we might earn and carry with us. We know it, Johnny. It is the little bird singing within and without. It is the perception that turns us, like homing pigeons, back to our birthright, to the primordial depth and beyond. It is that stupendous moment in which love resides. We double up, you and I, this man and woman within one being; we blend to make the one thing.

You sing to all of us, "The campfire glows; the wolf howls; the note taker is dead; the man speaks, the woman smiles. Is it our precious time, the fleeting chance, the possibility of human excellence? Protect your being. Seek long. Blend only with truth. I don't need to say it. All of this is what you are. I am listening too. We stretch ourselves across the stars."

Much love, my Johnny,
Your Olivia

Renascence

There are many stories—to hear a gentler one than this, we must earn it. You can try an antique, leather-bound book on the Renaissance full of riches, but the cosmos demands the oblique. The rhythms of life demand discrimination. The broad gestures of language can only hope to be generous. My travels are inward now, connected with something electrical: the light bulb burning in the empty kitchen, the gas stove burning the edges of the fat pizza, the burning starlight, the dull eyes of Deliberator, the blind stallion racing across the field. The stallion is satisfied in his travels across the field. He will stop at the fence on a dime. He is burning or cold at the shiver of a mare, or a fat cob of corn. He is only a stallion. He looks to breed his mare, Dusty Dream, as his kind have looked for a thousand years. I am not a blind stallion. I doubt that my friend Candice is a blind mare? I do not look for loving arms today. I do not choose another since my loved-one has gone away. The pizza is in the oven, and starlight is seething at the edge of the cheese. Candice is coming to lunch.

Singing. This song happens in the key of change. If it offends, know that it is merely words in transit engaging experience beyond the thought.

Do Candice and I travel upstream in the same boat? What other boat is there? And yet, she is looking for someone to be her own. Might I choose to talk of a relationship spanning time. Might I be strong in what I say, maybe very strong; for as I have found it, travel inward beyond the mundane can have an edge.

But wait! The moments come and go… Candice wheels in. Her red car sweeps down the lane, a quarter mile away, makes fresh tracks in the deep, sparkling snow. Candice. A young woman I've known only little while. Maybe twenty-eight, she is. A success with her own company, a painter in her spare time. Landscapes.

I have been sifting through books to clarify the useless and left them scattered. Candice wants to know me, and I her, of course. If I leave the books out, will she be scanning titles, looking for a brand on me? Branded. Sizzling, permanent. Well, all right, you might say, people have got to look at something. But for today, no books. Let the pizza be enough for us, all vegetables in the snow-covered kitchen looking out over the empty, white, rolling, monastic hills of Kentucky. It is a warm, easy kitchen with an ancient, wooden table. Will she worry then if the vegetable knife decapitates a bug?

No, not Candice. She isn't like that. She is sensitive, not issue bound, and she is charming. Charming because she makes charm happen—courteous, bright, kind, seeking. Doomed, possibly, I think—as we all might be—as I sift through the books.

One eye on the window, I track her in the red car. She slides at the big curve, a long, graceful, slow motion slide to the ditch. Maybe she was testing the snow against her speed—having fun. Now in the ditch she revs it up—spinning—rich, black earth shoots from the back tires flying into the field. Back on the road, she is out to check the damage. From my perspective: dark red coat, bright red car, white field, black dirt—color and stillness. She drives on, curving toward me, slower now.

I imagine her thoughts by the thousands tumbling off in the wind: honey bees, five hundred Luna moths on the wing, birds of paradise, dying house flies toddling behind like penguins, a mantis with a mouth full of broken wings trying to pray, all drags against the wheels. We know them all. I meet her at the car. Hands in my pockets against the wind. Nimbly, she is out in a heartbeat, warm smile, a greeting of goodness, reaches to give me a gentle hug. I barely get my hands out of my pockets in time.

"Well, I'm here, nice place, this open country of yours."

We have been together a couple of times before, Candice and I. One night, talking along the edges of history, I mentioned the color black. In passing, only. Black absorbs the spectrum of light, takes it all in. Symbol of wisdom in some ancient circles, the resplendent inner state. Said no. Candice. Black represented evil, cruelty and darkness to her. Different tradition, different scholar, different book, different symbol. Candice and I, two people talking. Symbols! But what of the real thing?

We have chatted about everything from the roll of dice to the diffusion of intent. We went to a movie, tainted as usual, funny a bit. But there you go! Culture. She seems everything a man could want. I see her standing there in the snow like, well, like the Duchess of Earl: you know the Duke of the song, his loved-one—hair swept back, quick to laugh, curving tenderly in her tight winter coat.

In the house, I smell pizza and say, "pizza!" and run. She gets it, and is right behind me. I throw open the hot oven door. She tosses me her colorful, blue and green and saffron glove, and the pizza is saved in a heartbeat.

In by the fire while the pizza cools. She picks up a book and asks with her eyes, "What is this?"

"A poet," I say.

"I see by the cover," she says.

"Don't open it now," I say. "Better for another time." Too beautiful, I tell myself, as I set it aside for her, this book of poetry. The delicate romantic love between man and woman is too far along for us. We could lose ourselves in that mood. With space, could other roads unfold?

I am in a hickory chair by the open fire, and she is up looking about. She stops and turns her head toward me over her shoulder, as if I whispered her name. Her eyes smile to me, looking to weigh anchor. A light? Energy floating in the space? Are those her deep intentions? Now, she seems more a solid chandelier.

I could add warmth to this story for you, but warmth that might drug us, and in wearing off turn to ice. I could spend time with conversation over lunch, but instead I'll pass on her fugitive thought, like a finch at dawn, that the condition of people is not all it is cracked up to be, even the seeming best of it. She is beginning to turn inward. "What is the trip you are taking?" she asks again.

I could tell you of being with her on the big, golden sofa as the afternoon wore on, and how high her wool skirt hiked when she tucked her leg under her, how warm the wood fire, how compatible we were, how tenderly she kissed me on the cheek moments after her long, eloquent sentence describing the lace ice flows at the falls of Love Lake and how the sun beat upon them. How, in essence, she offers her warmth to me, herself…maybe just for holding each other closely. How yes rustles in us. How I lean back without accepting her lovely offer. No feeling of separation. Only I know I don't accept her willing gesture—silence awhile. We wait.

"What is this trip you're taking," she asks?

"You know what," I say. "Isn't it strange who we are."

"Very strange." She smiles.

"It occurs to me," I say, that people are made of their conditioning since childhood and before. What struggling person might have held them, brought them up, as they say? Good intentions, I ask, does it matter much? I ask: who bought their books, defined their words, offered them too much in the way of bad food and facts?

Who slaked their inborn, tender, loving thirst for peace with raw opinion, and with the dead end of chemicals like old man alcohol and the forces carried on smoke? Heirlooms of emotion drift from mind to mind, I say. The trivial intellect talks on and on. Born where, who from, to what club, religion? Random experience, mixed with a little honey, but not honey enough. Honey? A different food, I say.

"I suppose," she says.

And there is more. I say.

I talk about the animal within, and the false self that commands us without us commanding it. The preposterous fear and laziness within humanity, the senses unhinged, the ungainly carnivorous engagement with the intellect, emotion, food and sex, without understanding or finesse. The thousand and one degrees of murder, there within the thoughts. All in the course of a day, these thoughts, drifting in and out of the being, until the food of the soul flutters against a stone vase.

"Well," she says. "Some people more than others." She steams up a bit. Defensive. "This is not new."

And I agree with her, yes, not new, yet scattered, subdued, truncated. It is only the one who really listens, who acts upon the knowledge, who makes a tremendous, conscious effort as rare as peace. Pedantry like barnacles hangs upon human history—only the deep freshness of spring for one or so. Whole civilizations live and die, and only a few make the journey. I tell her.

"I think maybe you are arrogant, wasting time." She tells me.

I don't mind her words, though ease is better, but what can I do? She apologizes briefly, unconvincingly because of her darkening mood. But I know what she means, and I tell her so to ease the break between us: she didn't really think that of me, just of the ideas, all the talk of human struggle.

Quiet now. Maybe she's remembering her poor Aunt Betsy, who in her mind was a saint. Maybe she is thinking of herself and the good job she has done so far. Maybe she doubts them both. But it sinks in today, as it does with almost all of us, someday. She knows there is something missing; she knows there is weakness in herself; with her life before her eyes in an expanded second, maybe she shuffles over all the people she knows and finds them confused and struggling. They put forward at times their best face, their stiff upper lip, their faith in hope, their faith in their new shoes—but floundering.

"Ego," she says.

"It seems to me," I say, very gently this time. "That people use the weapons of the ego to fight the ego. And so, stalemate."

The afternoon is not going the way she had imagined it—edging up the avenue in her red car at the height of her poetic understanding in the rolling white, elegant, hills of Kentucky, engaging the warm, open fire and the homemade pizza and an equal of sorts, me; all the rhythms of her reality were tenderly opened to be confirmed. She is disappointed. This is hard, maybe even shallow to her, earthbound.

She says: "Doesn't everyone complain this way?

Thinking people? Your ideas are not so rare. Of course, we are up against it in an imperfect world."

She wants companionship today. Love the way she knows it. And now a moody day, chilled by the intellect. She is right, you know; why chill tenderness between people? Why? Answer that. Is there a time when that chill could be kindness?

"Ego." I say. "Too easy. It is deeper than a personal, imaginative view of that word. It seems to me that an in-depth change in the ego would be beyond the skill of definition in the mind, or a rendition of beauty, beyond carte blanche, beyond the magnificence of the northern lights or rose buds, beyond ecstasy."

"How about, beyond magniloquent wheelbarrows," she asks and smiles. "Are you a Surrealist?"

I laugh. "Beyond them, too." Yes, quick and funny—she is—good she decides to cut back at me. I don't answer her Surrealist parry. It isn't a moment for intellectual play. I could say: why go beyond the real anyway? I could point out that almost the whole world is surreal, and leave it at that. I don't. Too easy.

She becomes quiet again. It is one of those fine, sparse, uncompressed days, one of those days when it is possible to hear the faint, calming sounds of the distance: the warble of a yellow dog chanting to be free, the bluster of an invisible train.

She finally speaks, not so much to me as to the smoldering logs. "Am I a little harsh, too", she asks? "I know. I am. You are trying to talk about what we are like inside. Just that."

I say truly, yes, and my yes, softens things, I guess. She leans against me, her cascading hair against my neck; an ideal she is: thoughtful, warm, interested. No groveling over the pizza, even inwardly—abstemious, healthy. Her body begins to imprint her thin, soft, blue dress, nothing special, just ongoing in the warmth of the fire. Fresh. Her lips part slightly, her shoe falls from her foot to the floor.

I look at her against me. My feeling: respect, tremendously, like seeing a work of art in progress, but a greater thing, a human being struggling in that manner, a sculpture with invisible chips of stone flying away like startled birds into oblivion leaving only the essence, the truth, the immortal. The chisel allows the breeze to seep into the pores, deep into the cells, the kiss from the cause of life. Not mortal like a pizza or a winter coat, not dumb as they are dumb, not an idiot of faith or imagination.

I heave a cedar log into the fire. The sparks began to snap, the cat scurries, and I know she will gallop on to the kitchen to gnaw a crust of pizza from the table. But if I put her out today, well, she will get bred in a heartbeat—regularly, that drive, with nothing much in between but food and sleep.

I sit down again with Candice.

"There is a chance you will waste your life," I say.

She grabs for her shoe, quick, smooth, like catching a fly on the wing and looks straight into my eyes. Boldly, ankle to knee, hem of dress falling to her thighs, shoe to foot. Internally, on her way out the door. She catches herself. I'm not surprised. She is too smart to miss anything, to let chances to learn go by, and not thin-skinned, not weak like the run of the mill.

"You don't get off so easy." She leans back and smiles. She had gathered her aplomb in a heartbeat. Nothing fake about it. "You are going on a trip. Or did you say you've been? We have brought this up several times. You don't tell where or why? Tell me now."

I say. My trip? I am not going where the cat goes, I tell Candice, or where the fine, dun mare wants to go, which is to the feedbag or to the stallion or to sleep. Most of the day the cat likes to torture and kill and devour and sleep. People can sleep all of the day and do their dirty work consuming in a somnambulist trance. Rather like us. She flinches, restraint, she listens. The cat would be as fat as a swine eating its carrion if I would let her. If I would let her, the beautiful, dun mare would eat until her legs would lock into pegs and she would jerk along on all fours like a frozen spider—"foundered" as they say on the farm. Tears would come to the dun mare's eyes. And the cat would cry softly. If they were given all of what they want.

I say. We try to understand the cat and the dun mare, and take care of them. It is people who have the capacity for consciousness. If we are foundered, we can cure it. When the cosmos loves us, we can see our hidden faults and turn against them. Who can change to become lovable in that invisible realm? Our trip is not the trip of the animal, so we must know our history, our resume of muscle and blood. The trip is the trip that nobody takes. Yet someone will—always—because it can be done, I propose to her.

She leans toward me; she holds her ground with the strength of her mind. There is an unnatural steadiness in her eyes. She puts her hand on my knee showing me she isn't afraid. Her eyes go soft, as if the imprint of some fresh Mona Lisa was coming through, but distantly, not for me. She doesn't really like me anymore.

She starts to speak. She stops. Her hand is on my knee. Light years stretch away leaving only the moment. Warmth. Thin, silver bracelet at her wrist. Beauty. In that gentle hand, wrist bent as if holding a brush, afternoon peace.

She says: "How about if we just hold each other? How about that, tenderly, with respect and love. We can drink dark tea, talk of the ups and downs of childhood. We can discuss religion and poetic living and take a walk in these empty hills. Love would freshen around us and we could talk of houses with white blossoms. How about it? We could start with holding each other, maybe just kiss the afternoon away."

Tears well into her eyes. They are wet with tears, brimming. She brushes them away with the hand that had been on my knee. She seems to have gone too far into the emotions she has mothered so long, too far into that intuitive sense of what is missing from the mundane.

She hears the soft tick of the iron clock and it jolts her. Somewhere in her heart she knows the whisper of something completely whole, entirely beautiful that must be found within. She holds her hand gently at her neck as if closing the collar of a coat against a cold wind.

Inside I know, "I love her". Love for an exceptional woman intending passionately to be true. I love her for who she is, for what she has done. I love her for what she someday might become. To her I say "All you feel and say is beautiful," I mean it deeply and she knows it.

She's up and moves closer to the fire with a clumsy turn of her body as if too many words have cut off her circulation. All the talk has cut off mine. I stretch, and take a deep, slow breath. She turns her back to me, watches the fire. She is thinking.

"You know what I am tired. I don't know how to be with you," she says. "I am tired of ideas that have piled up, that can go nowhere today, tired of talk, tired of losing this beautiful December afternoon. I'm leaving. Don't walk me out. But with your permission I will walk out and sit on the hill out there." She turns to the window, her back to me. "If you don't mind, I would like to be there alone before I go." I nod my assent. For her, I want everything. She is everyone.

"Of course," I say. At that, she gathers that dark red, sleek, form-fitting, wool coat and is out the door in a heartbeat.

I step out, too. Smoke tree holding a leaf. Gray. Winter. Night falling from far away. The light, like rest. The horses will be waiting as is their habit. Now and then the cat bounds from footprint to footprint, or trots along beside me on the white, white frozen snow. She is a good mouser, happy, always alert and interested, never bored.

The dun mare, Dusty Dream, is against the fence waiting for me. She holds in profile like a bronze statue, a streak of alabaster against the snow, but a statue for a moment only. Nickering in that deep, tender voice, shifting from foot to foot, the clear, winter breeze touching her mane, her head rising and falling, whirling with her ears back to scatter the restless mares waiting behind her, and making the full circle with a kind expression, ears up for me. I lean my head against hers, my cheek against her cheek, and we are still for a moment. As I carry in the bale of grass hay, she nuzzles me aside for the first fleck. Gently. A fine mare, strong, involved.

Deliberator! There he is, the huge, blind, black thoroughbred stallion. Blind, with a stallion's beauty of the highest. Is the dun mare more beautiful? Watching her, well, yes, but.... What is beauty? Love itself? So then. His tail, long and full and dark, brushes the white snow. Perfectly formed he is, no weight but what he needs for peace. He knows I am near. He whirls and lifts his front feet into the air and whirls again and makes for the fence at a gallop—no sight for the bare trees, the violet sky, the jagged fences and the drunken hills—they go on forever—no sight for the winter day—completely within, he comes charging.

I scan the horizon to freshen my view of the evening, I see Candice in the far distance, a little, dark red brush stroke. I try to forget her in this time with the horses. Naturally I miss her, but I turn from her now. Nothing harsh. Let her be.

Deliberator slides to a stop—the fence—his chest bowing in the plank, snow powdering the air, pure and true—the snow—as the sparkles float and fall and remain in me fresh forever. I throw the hay. He knows it. He waits. He swings away and swings back. Dancing. He is fun loving, inclines to joy. He is dancing. To play. Naturally. He waits until I touch his face. I pat his face and smooth his long wild, elegant forelock. He has no fear, no haste. He cares deeply for this moment, and every other. I rub his nose on both sides with my open hands. He lifts his head sharply and looks over my shoulder. He cannot see, and yet.... He leans back into my hands, gently. I brush his cheeks and around his eyes with my hand. In time he steps away. No division. He is awake when others sleep. He is blind to the things of the day. Inside he is all sparkles soothing him, like snow sparkles hanging languidly in the evening air. He is old. I have known him all of my life. And these are the things that he whispered to me over the long years, forever.

A year passes. Again it is December. Again. Snow. In that I have lived fully, retreated for some of my needs, come forward for others. A year can be a long, engaging time for some of us. Again a violet sky. All different, all better. Following that same timeless lead. Love? Let it be nameless, that force. Naturally. Strong. I feel. As always now, detaching from the dross. Coming up from the barn I see the cat against a pane of glass that must be a hundred years old, the waves in the glass give her a diffuse air, as if maybe she is dying and going away. But none the less for wear in that journey. Naturally. She declined to trot with me to the barn because of the bitter wind

I come to the door. There is a note from Candice. I have to think twice. I have not seen her, nor heard of her, since that day she left me in the afternoon, long ago. It is folded and says, "from Candice." I take off my glove to unfold it. In fresh ink it reads:

Come on out the ridge
And find me,
I'll be the one in the black coat
On the white hill
With a sleigh.

In a heartbeat, I begin to think. She is stepping into another room. That room is on her way to becoming uncluttered. Her coat, the one she wears, might be any color, a brush of red, but she paints it black for me in her poem—the resplendent inner, symbolic black of which we chatted. Her hill is pure, and that is the white thought of which she speaks, not cold snow forever melting. I'll make a bet there is no sleigh; she speaks instead of action, an effort onward. She invites me to join her in that trip. Sustenance between us, naturally. Yes, she'll be out there alone, no little sleigh, I'll bet; I'll wager the symbolic fortune in my pocket: a piece of string, my pet frog, her sleigh, and the little raft I fashion to head out with her on the broad Mississippi.

The Love That Was Missouri

The tall woman beside me was the only one of the four of us who was at ease on this Island of Death. She wore blue jeans ripped at the hip by the blade of a tramp. Tramp is a technical term that refers loosely to those who roam here without depth in values or conscience, for the adventure of roaming, and will kill for what they want. It could be for a piece of clothing, a plate of food, a weapon, a political advantage or the coarse fulfillment of a whim—to name a few clear nouns at the core. However, the tall woman with the wonderful smile killed the tramp with two fingers at the vein of his delicate throat.

We topped the hill above the bright Mississippi, silently, to make for a footbridge that crossed a wide fissure. With a rough hold on her arm from the back, I saw Gordon, his sleeves rolled above his biceps, stop his wife Jenna in her tracks. The tall woman saw, too, and held like a statue.

And yet I took another step, my shoulder accidently touching hers, and froze with her; I could feel her breathing. Briefly I saw the pain reflect in Jenna's face from the unconscious grip Gordon held at her arm. He looked tensely across the hundred yards to the river's edge.

There at the edge of the river was a boy, twelve perhaps, with a scalar gun fastened to the top of his wrist behind the hand. The arm was up and out, the hand relaxed forward as it might look if the wrist were broken, and the arm swept the landscape gracefully, like the arm of a dancer or the body of a snake, sure sign that the boy was proficient and at ease with the weapon. In his other hand he held a long cane fishing pole. His trousers were rolled up to the knees; on his head was an old straw hat. He glanced from the landscape he swept with the scalar weapon back to the cork bobbing in the bright waters of the Mississippi.

Slowly the four of us, almost as one, bent at the knees and sunk behind the ridge of the hill. Over the rough grass we crawled quietly together. There's no way to reach the bridge without him seeing. "There's no way to reach the bridge without him seeing us," Gordon said. He released his grip on Jenna's arm; his cool tone and the realities of the life then made it clear that he had swiftly and not unreasonably condemned the boy to death. I waited.

"He's just a boy," Jenna said.

"One touch to the trigger would mean the four of us," Gordon said. He was looking at me.

"Scalar gun," I said to Jenna.

"Oh," Jenna said.

The tall woman was silent. Gordon and I were scientists on this crazed Island of Missouri. Since the fissures had opened up around us, we, like all the other scientists at the International Conference—coded "Review"—were trapped. And so was everyone.

Three years had passed, a culture had grown up, if you can call it that, in which among many, aberrance, cruelty, disease, and unbridled imagination spread with rapidity. And among a few, shall we call them—The stable? The thoughtful? The kind? — ways were found to cope and create, and along with that challenge to discover, to find a way out. The fissures that made Missouri an island seemed impassable. This was so not only because of their incredible width and depth, but also because the outside was keeping us in. Who was outside? What government? We no longer knew. We hypothesized; we made jokes, but who could know? One theory was that early after the Great Disturbance, as we called it, someone had managed to get out and had revealed the presence of the Diseased People (another technical term) and the nature of their infirmity, possibly distorted out of proportion—a scientist with a grudge perhaps. Atomic Break Walls had been set up around the Island on the far sides of the fissures so that no communications came to us nor were able to leave. All aircraft were either exploded or disintegrated by unseen weapons at the far edge of the ocean of air that surrounded us. Even the big colorful balloons, red and green, that we launched into that air, popped silently and winked out.

"We'll have to kill him," Gordon said without emotion, his expression relaxing after weighing all the factors. Of course, I wasn't surprised.

"He's just a boy," Jenna said again. "He's fishing."

"There are no damn fish in the river," Gordon hissed. "Why is he there? I think he's hunting; he's probably the son of a rich tramp judging from his weapon. And we're fair game.

"There could be fish in the river," I said. "Remember the Michael James project?"

"Michael James is crazy. He'll never purify the river."

"Maybe," I said.

"Okay," Gordon said. "I don't care if there are jewels in that river, the kid with the weapon has got to go. We have only so much daylight; there is no way but the bridge.

"The tall woman broke in; her manner was calm; her tone was final. "He's fishing," she said.

We all looked at her in surprise, Gordon with

something extra in his narrowed eyes; disagreement to that heart meant encounter. He was ready. We didn't know the tall woman. She had been with us only thirty minutes. By killing the Tramp she had saved our lives. We had been moving through the narrow streets of the Empty Section to avoid being seen, to avoid death, from building to building, our guns trained on doors and windows we moved like warm steel, but not one of us had seen the stone blind built by the Tramps. The tall woman had been coming the other way alone and the two Tramps watching us had not seen her until she was against the roofless structure of stone. She called out to us, "People, watch, watch!" Such a formal warning, but as long as I live I'll never forget the timber of her voice, the true love there, her concern shining through like the track of a tear,

"People, watch, watch!" In moments, she closed her right hand deftly on the throat of a Tramp, and I killed the other with one shot to the spine.

Gordon, without a thought, answered her with contempt, "How could you know he is fishing?" That was Gordon.

"He's read Huckleberry Finn and he's fishing," the tall woman said calmly. "He's innocent and we don't have to kill him."

"You're crazy," said Gordon. He put his hand to his forehead in his accustomed gesture, as if the weight of the world bore against his brain.

"Huckleberry Finn is popular among the children of the book people," the tall woman continued. "It's one of the few recent books recovered and passing among them. That boy is dressed like Huck Finn, his jeans are rolled up; he is wearing a straw hat. It is a costume, I can tell. He has a cane pole. There is no other sense to it. Why would a Tramp be hunting like that, exposed on the riverbank? Then the tall woman added, "I'm sorry, do you know the book I'm talking about?"

"I haven't read it," Gordon answered through clenched teeth. "I'm not in the habit of spending time with trivia, but I know damn well what you mean, and I think it's crazy. And I don't think you are in a position to suggest what we do."

"Gordon," Jenna exclaimed with unaccustomed force. "This woman saved your life."

"There are four of us now," I said. Gordon just shrugged and stared at me.

Gordon and I were as close as we could ever be it seemed. He loved me as a friend and he would listen to me, but he felt I was too soft, not tough enough for a scientist and a survivor on this confused and bloody island. We both had our feelings, but it was theory that was important to Gordon, and now it was the theories of the events that led to the upheavals that pleased him to discuss. Yet, I was growing a little cool to retrospective theory; but to see the boy with the scalar weapon strapped to his wrist, nuclear underground testing seemed so primitive and the grossness of the bombs, so solemnly detonated, so clear. And the enormous electromagnetic pulse (EPM) that accompanied those blasts was absorbed by the huge bulk of the planet. The 4.2 x 10 joules of energy 3 (1 joule = .2390 calorie) released by every one megaton blast in the first four billionths of a second was absorbed as well. As you can see the effect of a five-megaton blast was considerable. The crust of Nevada is only about 35 kilometers thick. Maybe it still is, in some fashion or another, who knows? But from the crust the EPM shock wave became an MHD wave (magneto hydrodynamic) and traveled through the more reactive mantle. It moved as a disturbance down to the core/mantle interface where blast after blast was remembered. Just maybe that was one factor. And Missouri isn't the same anymore.

Gordon watched me, waiting for me to respond. I looked through him, and thought of the boy fishing in the ancient Mississippi. I thought of the boy alone at night like so many boys, in the one hundred years gone by, living within the life of old Huck Finn, just as a boy, not as history, barefoot with sunburned cheeks and torn trousers, in his time and in his place, all bright and young and thoughtful. Then I caught myself; maybe it was all crazy; what did the tall woman know? I looked at her. Alert, she was watching me.

She said: "Did you see the way he watched his cork?"

"No," I said. I hadn't noticed.

"Time," Gordon snarled. "Time."

"I'm not afraid of the boy," Jenna said softly. Then she smiled at the tall woman.

"I won't bet my life on a dime novel against a gun," Gordon said. His finger touched a switch and a tiny light on the side of his weapon flashed once and went out. He started to rise up.

"Could I talk to the boy," the tall woman asked. "If I fail, I die, then he is yours."

"Suicide," Gordon whispered. He knew I would speak if I wished to speak. I was quiet.

"Be quick," he said to her.

The tall woman stood up and raised her arms above her head like some ancient temple dancer. I scooted up on my belly so that I had a view of the boy, my cheek flat in the grass. I knew that if he pulled the trigger without warning that I would die too, but I felt something true in the deed of the tall woman and I was impelled to watch as if that would support her. Only as an afterthought did I train my weapon on the boy.

"Boy," the tall woman called out. Her arms were still above her head, the wrists rigid, the palms flat and facing out as if she was holding something away from her in the air. She was careful not to let her hands fall at the wrists and give the impression of a scalar weapon. The boy was as still as a bird of prey, the arm out, the wrist arched, fingers down, the tall woman in his sights. Behind him he held the long cane pole lazily out over the water. His hair was gold in the light, sundown.

"My weapon is behind me on the ground," the tall woman called out. "My name is Olivia. I only want to cross the bridge to your right. I did not kill you because I thought you were truly fishing."

"I am fishing," said the boy. He didn't move, cool and still.

"You know of Huckleberry Finn," said the tall woman.

Surprised, his face softened. "I know him," he said.

"I know him too," said the woman. "How deep are you fishing?"

"Deep? What do you mean, deep?"

"How far is it from your cork to your hook?"

"One foot."

"Make it three feet and you will do better. I have fished before."

"You don't look that old," said the boy.

"I am," said the tall woman.

"Are you alone?"

"My friends are behind me on the ground. They are afraid of your weapon."

I was becoming transfixed by her voice. Beauty? What is it? That was in her voice. "You may cross the bridge," the boy said.

"My friends will be afraid to trust you," said the tall woman. "Tell them why you are going to let them cross."

"Why? What do you mean?"

"Tell them who you are and why you are here, why you have that weapon." The boy hesitated. The tall woman held her arms unmoving in the air.

"Just talk and there will be no reason to kill."

"I am here because I read about fishing and I want to try it. I am here because my Mother is dead and because my Father is a scientist who wants to change this place and he works and I can slip away."

"Why do you have the weapon?"

"I have it to kill anyone who tries to get me. My Father made it. We have more."

"Gordon's voice came from behind me. He spoke to the tall woman.

"I know his Father. Let's stop the talking and get to the bridge."

"My friends will stand up; they will carry their weapons over their heads until they reach the bridge."

The boy was weaving his weapon hand gently as we stood up and moved without hesitation toward the fissure and the bridge. The tall woman waited to let us pass.

"I'm going to pick up my weapon now," the tall woman said.

"By the way, how old are you?"

"I'm eleven," said the boy, his voice now cold as he concentrated his weapon on our movement.

"It is very good that you are interested in reading," the tall woman said. "You will learn much. Have you read

Tom Sawyer?"

The boy's voice brightened like the ringing of a small, fine bell. "You mean there is a book about him too? Have you seen it?"

"I've seen it," she said. "You can find it at Number 7 on Street Sheen in the Full Quarter. Describe me and you will find friends. Forget my name."

She moved away from the boy and was soon close behind me as I stepped on to the bridge. I felt warmth, a safety, even a joy, as she moved in behind me with her weapon high above her head. And I knew the boy with his weapon trained loosely upon us was missing her and wishing in his feeling that she could sit beside him on the river bank and tell what she knew, string pearls for him about the wide Mississippi.

Midway across the bridge we could no longer see the boy. In my mind I saluted him, goodbye. Moments later as I stepped from the bridge my state was altered, safety not even a memory, warmth not even a word, joy a joke, for the bridge was watched: a hunting ground for the lowly. Eleven men with primitive lasers lifted themselves from shallow pits and called for us to hold. They were behind our left shoulders; no time to turn and fire. Gordon jerked to turn, a shot was fired meant to kill him but missed. He froze and lifted his weapon above his head. Silence. Why didn't they fire? And then I knew. They wanted the women alive.

"We will not kill you," one of their number called out. A lie. I would have to take a chance and fire.

"Just lay your weapons down slowly."

I hesitated. From the corner of my eye I saw the red scarf of the tall woman. She stood on the tip of the bridge. Slowly she lowered her weapon to the ground. From some sort of trust building in me toward her, incredibly I too began to lay my weapon down. Immediately there was a live click in the air, as if the click surrounded us, or it was a sensation, as if lightning had struck without light and without thunder. The eleven men became a sort of dust that drifted for a half second on the wind and was gone. The tall woman was already lifting her hand in thanks across the fissure.

The boy was leaning against a rock. His straw hat was pushed back on his head; his arm and the scalar weapon he had just fired hung at his side. He had killed eleven men, decadent men, men of death. He was defending a world of innocence and love. He seemed weary, stunned in the way children seem to get after a long, long day.

Consider the rain forests. Would you prefer Africa or the more mysterious Amazon? Consider them well. All the golden birds and the red ones, the flowers and the flies, the green-eyed animals and the sounds they make, and the rivers, The Maranon and The Japura. And the people, some with painted faces, and others in the government, all of them cutting trees. Consider the singing of the pavos and the eagle, the whippoorwill and the quail, consider the leaves of the palm. Choose Africa or the Amazon, dream of deer or armadillo or campfires. All of this matters in Missouri. At least it mattered once.

As a scientist I was asserting that deforestation be controlled, that trees be a priority of the planet. Was I too late? Were my assertions wrong, out of date with new research. Trees metabolize vast quantities of CO_2. I realized, as did many others that the rain forests of the world were one of the greatest sinks for that substance. I realized that the early droughts in Africa were not merely currents in a cycle. A CO_2 imbalance breeds desert. Africa is not isolated; the Amazon is not an anomaly. Dry winds now blow across Missouri.

"Why are you frowning," the tall woman asked? It was getting dark and our danger was very great. I was walking just behind her and when she turned our faces were near. We had stopped while Gordon reconnoitered around a blind curve.

"I was thinking about trees," I said.

"Trees?" she said. She looked at me closely

"Palms, myrtles, laurels, acacias, cedrelas, cecropias, rosewood, bombacaceae, fig, mimosa, millions of them."

"What about the trees?" She watched me.

"They cut too many of them."

"Yes, that's true," she said. "That's part of our problem here." This time I met her stare. It was clear; it gave the sense that she already knew me, not my name, but something more important to us both.

"Why did you stay with us," I asked?

Jenna was sitting on the ground a few yards away. We heard a stick break in the trees. Instinctively the tall woman and I turned back-to-back and rotated slowly, straining our eyes to catch any hint of danger. Side by side again, we waited.

"I stayed with you for two reasons," she said, as if there had been no break. "One. I recognized you and I know your project."

I was shocked, more than a little unnerved. Only one other man knew of our project. He was a hermit and a genius and my friend. He had helped us with some of the calculations, but had no interest in taking part. He was old and elegant and wise.

"Yes, he told me," she said, as if reading my

thoughts. “He is my friend as well. I also use to take him food and talk to him by the hour. He told me of your project because he trusts me and knowing that you could take a fourth person he encouraged me to find you and your people.”

“But how did you do it?”

“By wanting to do it, it happened. These things do happen, don’t they?”

“But you’ve never seen me before.”

“You were described. So was the ring you wear on your left hand.”

“But the odds, we weren’t even supposed to be in that area… ” Her look interrupted me. That look was not interested in odds, but penetrating and patient, it accepted the fact.

“I am here,” she said.

Gordon appeared in the half-light and motioned us forward. I gave Jenna a hand up. Again we walked in single file, two looking left and two looking right, weapons ready.

The house was on a hill covered with morning glories. Something had given them the edge. It was then that we heard the screams and the firing. Never had we seen so many of the Diseased People together. The one thing about them that no one could figure was why they moved without attacking each other. Deranged, demented, short-lived, they attacked anything that moved: people, animals, bushes, trees, the leaves that blew across the ground, and yet they could distinguish and plan in most stages of their decline, and other people were their preferred prey. Those caught were cannibalized. They became diseased in this way by simply eating the wrong food. The protections were simple, everyone knew what to avoid and what to add to the diet, but as with most everything there were people who had no will, no restraint. Some moved alone, others in "packs."

The screaming was terrible; there must have been forty of the Diseased People attacking a group of about ten Tramps. The Tramps had killing lights mounted on their shoulders, lights that went on with a touch to a switch on a weapon, then off again after the firing. They must have had our house staked out for a kill when the Diseased People came, and now they were fighting for their lives with spring knives, primitive homemade blades that were fired with a spring, used by those who could neither buy nor steal a better weapon.

We had to get to our house behind the wire. We had made an intricate barricade of "cutting wire" which was electrified with a camouflaged lift that could raise a section for our entry. All of us knew that this terrible fighting might draw others, hungry to the kill, and without hesitation we walked toward the house. The Tramps were blinking on and off like crazed fireflies and this strobe effect lit the Diseased in a strange staggering.

The screams were a blend that gurgled, and as we angled in toward the edge of the yard a wave of the Diseased saw us and came charging. Jenna was the only one who fired from the hip and she was quick and deadly at close range.

We shot at shadows and with rapidity in the flashes of the killing lights, but I feared for us and fought desperately. Two of the Diseased were on Gordon's back screaming like monkeys. The tall woman and I turned and fired, a chance we took without a thought, and the two fell dead. Gordon moved forward and reached the wire. Where was Jenna? I moved swiftly to my right in the dark and saw in the flash of a light that she was being dragged backward in the arm of a Tramp with a lock on her neck. Though we were saving their lives, there was not depth enough to resist the cruel capture of a woman. I moved around him in the dark, and though I hated it, I cut his throat. Gordon was at the wire with the lift open; the tall woman was watching us while turning in a circle as graceful as a dancer spinning, her weapon firing its beams. Then she was surrounded; I saw Gordon move for better position to help her. And then it seemed I saw two figures go through the lift opening in the wire. Jenna and I moved swiftly to the rescue of the tall woman, needing position to fire, and soon the four of us moved toward the opening and went through. Behind us, as the lift went down, three forms were left writhing in the sparks of the cutting wire.

In the living room Gordon threw a match in the fire and it flamed up. He turned around flushed with anger.

"Pleasant world we live in isn't it? Is anyone one surprised?" Jenna and I were quiet, too exhausted to get into it with Gordon.

"No," the tall woman said calmly. "I'm not surprised."

"You must be a scientist or something," Gordon replied with sarcasm.

"Something like that," the tall woman said.

The house was spacious and comfortable. I had my own room with a suspended bed and a great window looking out over the river. I offered it to the tall woman for which she thanked me and went there with the small shoulder bag in which she carried her things. Actually, she wasn't such a tall woman. I noticed when we were near in the house that she was a couple of inches shorter than I was; it was the way she held herself, her bearing made her seem tall.

Gordon immediately began work on the propulsion mechanism for the Silver Shuttle. He didn't speak a word to Jenna other than to give her orders. When I told him the woman was coming with us he said simply, "There's room." Toward midnight the area around the house was quiet and, of course, there would be no bodies to carry away. Jenna was sewing by the fire, the tall woman standing by the window, when Gordon stood up cursing. "I can't be ready by tomorrow. It will be another forty days before the satellite will pass again." We had to have those signals.

"And forty nights," said Jenna. "If we have to wait we have to wait, why be so miserable?"

"The hell with you and your satisfaction, I work until I work until I can't move, and you…."

"There is another factor," the tall woman broke in. "Have you heard of the project, Scalar Sweep?"

"We've heard," I said. "That's Dr. Brune. We thought it was a joke, impossible at this time."

"It is no longer a joke; he has the technology and he's gone into hiding. People are looking for him, but it is not too complicated a matter to build what he needs. If he's not found, it could be tomorrow, it could be next week, and no more Missouri, a clean sweep to the fissures. He's convinced others to help him who do so with the zeal of those fanatics who mix emotion, religion and politics so they can hurt people with conviction."

"What does this mean," Jenna asked?

"It means," Gordon said. "That the man is building a broad-based scalar which he will trigger and kill all living things in Missouri in a matter of seconds. But don't worry, Jenna, with your thick skin you'll be sure to live through it." Jenna lowered her eyes to her sewing. She always hid them as they would fill so quickly with tears.

"Gordon," I said quietly. "Jenna doesn't have a thick skin."

"I'm sorry," he said. "I'm sorry, Jenna." He turned and left the room.

"It's the pressure," Jenna said. "He doesn't really mean it." She picked up her sewing, a golden shirt with trees—green and golden palms—and followed after him. I felt a light touch at my arm.

"My name is Olivia," she smiled. I felt myself smiling too. It felt very good. "You forgot I had a name, didn't you?"

"I forgot that I could smile."

"Come into my room, the one you gave me, and let's relax awhile. I've made a special tea."

She had a candle burning and the moon was sparkling over the wide river. She had changed into a soft shirt that shone a little like a polished silk. Her hair was down about her shoulders and the chiseled features of her face were soft too, beautiful and kind. It was all a little too much for me considering the constant struggles, considering that only moments before I had perceived only a warrior woman without a name.

"My name is Jake," I said.

We sat on the floor by the low window drinking a tea that was strange and soothing. The night was so clear that I thought I might see a fish jump, if fish there were.

"What was the second reason you came with us," I asked. "You said there were two."

"You were the second reason, and Jenna, and maybe Gordon too." Her gaze was steady; it made me uncomfortable.

"I know that at any moment we could die."

"The scalar of Dr. Brune?"

"Yes, that." She spoke tentatively.

"The ride in the Silver Shuttle?"

"That too." Her voice was the same.

"But what else."

"You forgot natural causes." At that she smiled. I was confused. She laughed and said that the last part was sort of a joke, but not completely. And that yes, the scalar was the most likely. She said that forty days and forty nights was a good period of time to get something done if we lasted that long. Her manner was easy; she was relaxed, but there was something in her tone, a force in her manner that let me know that she meant for me to listen.

"But what is there to get done?"

"You mentioned the Michael James project."

Yes, I said that I had mentioned it. It was a project to purify the river, but that I knew nothing about the techniques and that he was using boats and specialized equipment which we didn't have. She listened intently.

"So, how could I purify the river?"

She looked at me for a few seconds and then with a quizzical expression she asked:

"What about yourself?"

"Myself, how could I without the equipment, oh, you mean…" She nodded, still with that questioning look.

"You mean," I repeated slowly. "To purify myself?"

She nodded yes, and now she was looking at me with a hard stare, a piercing stare, that told me that whatever I thought, she herself meant what she said. I had heard of such things and I associated statements like that with the ebb and flow of cults across the earth, with so-called gurus and other confused thinkers with something to sell. I've never been against what is pure; I've taken care of myself, but this was too much. I was tired; I couldn't take it. And yet, I felt like I could sit with her forever.

"I'm tired," I said. I stood up. She didn't look at me. She seemed to be looking out across the river. I said: "Couldn't we talk about this another time?" In a level matter-of-fact tone she asked: "What other time have you got?"

I turned to leave the room.

"You can sleep in here on the floor," she said. I kept walking. I don't remember saying good night.

The next day we all had breakfast together. Gordon was in a better mood and was cordial to everyone. Olivia acted as if nothing had happened between us. She was charming. She seemed to glow and attract us all. Jenna was happy to have a friend and they laughed and cooked together, even made a pie out of some sweet potatoes we had grown. I helped them with the pie.

Gordon had built a fire and soon we were sitting around it with warm cups of Olivia's soothing tea.

"How was sleeping on the hard floor," Jenna asked me. Before I could answer Olivia said, "I told him to sleep in my room on the floor, the rug is thicker and more comfortable." I looked at her; I felt something coming from a world foreign to me.

"Well you should have," Jenna said, giving me a wink that she knew Olivia would see.

"I think I offended Jake a little last night," Olivia continued. "I didn't mean to."

"Jake's not easily offended," Jenna replied. "Are you Jake?"

"Not really."

"This all sounds a little mysterious," Jenna said with a twinkle. "I think I'd like to hear what was so offensive."

"Tell her, Olivia," I said, feeling safe and distant, but as soon as I heard her voice begin I wished I had kept quiet.

"I told Jake that at any moment we might die and I asked him if he had ever thought of what it meant to purify oneself."

Gordon had been watching the fire, relaxed and half listening, probably interweaving thoughts of his theories of the upheavals; but when he heard this, he sat bolt upright and looked at Olivia with narrowed eyes. Jenna felt this tension, but she liked the woman, and I could tell that she trusted her too and wanted to know what she meant.

"That's not so offensive," Jenna said trying to gather her good humor. "And of course we might die, for a number of reasons, the scalar project for one, and who could object to a little cleaning up. Is this religion or health or philosophy or what?"

"It has to do with other levels of spirit. And awareness," Olivia said. Again she seemed to be the tall woman without a name.

"Oh," said Jenna.

"Hell fire," said Gordon. "When will I ever be left alone? I'm going to the turret." He left. We had a makeshift armored turret from which we could view and sweep clean the hillside surrounding the house. We also had armored plate in the walls and armored shutters for the windows.

"You'll have to understand Gordon," Jenna said to Olivia. "Don't judge him to harshly; he's never spent a lot of time understanding people."

"I know what you mean, I won't judge him. I like him already." Her voice was clear and tender and she meant what she said. Jenna smiled warmly and put her hand over Olivia's.

"Now tell us about this spirit," Jenna said.

The woman, Olivia, talked so that talking became something else: a rhythm, a song, the thought behind the song, the singer, pieces of sound, poetry that gathered up the time and spread it like rain. She spoke of people with names I had never heard, desert people and mountain people, and told us what they had said. She asked questions that were never answered and asked those that were answers in themselves. Her telling was a movement, trance-like, direct—an experience as real as snow or sunlight. She spoke of purity, not as an idea, but as a force that allowed a force that was real. She spoke of Huck Finn and his loyalty. She spoke of another kind of loyalty connected to the loyalty that moved Huck to be true. It could exist in our work and all we do, and as the truth we feel in wild nature. She spoke of Mark Twain and how he must have had something more than mere intellect to know the words to clear the brush away. She spoke of gratitude and how it must exist in a human being to allow things to happen of a higher nature: gratitude to people, and for being alive and existing to discover, for all the gifts of the universe, for the opportunity to grow and learn. Two hours passed as nothing to us, and she talked about the breath and the life contained within it.

We enjoyed talking about Mark Twain and Huck Finn, and they made us laugh and feel happy on and on, until they became a recurring part of the stream of our time, and we laughed often at other jokes, asking, "Would Mark Twain have thought that funny?" And finally, with the breath, she showed us a technique of breathing and we were doing it in a way that, with all that had penetrated into our feeling, it seemed as if our life had taken a turn toward something clear and indispensable. While we were doing the breathing with our eyes closed Gordon came down from the armored turret.

As we heard his footsteps we opened our eyes and a strange thing took place, strange even to me, a scientist, for he responded in a way that I never seen in the years I had known him. He responded to a gathering, invisible force. He became soft and receptive. He bumped into the edge of the table, smiled and plopped down in an empty chair.

"Why's everyone so quiet," he said almost to himself. And then without waiting for an answer, "Sure is nice to get out of that turret, I was beginning to think like a sardine." We all burst into wild laughter and Gordon was laughing until tears ran down his cheeks. He caught his breath long enough to blurt out, "Boy, you all are in a good mood." And then he was shaking with laughter again. To realize the state we were in when he entered the room and to know Gordon and his ways was enough in that moment to convince me of something hidden, of something that moved beyond the visible. Something that touched even Gordon.

At that moment the front door flew open and slammed against the wall, and there, swollen and slobbering like a pig was one of the Diseased in tatters with a stick of wood in his hand. He slammed the wood into the side of the door and it splintered. I leaped for the back door and threw it open. I screamed, "Out, out," and grabbed Jenna by the shoulder and actually threw her out the door. Gordon and Olivia went next and I followed hearing the shriek as the person charged. Gordon had fallen over Jenna but they rolled out of the way; I spun back toward the door, and as the man came out I hit him a blow in the kidney and then with one foot pushed him into the wire and he was finished.

Immediately I heard the voice of the Tramp. He was dressed in tight-fitting hunting pants and expensive leather boots. He wore a silk shirt and suede gloves and held a late model S4 pistol in his right hand. He was handsome and spoke in a casual manner.

"Seems you didn't like my little friend I let under the wire to visit you, but death has many faces and I'm not one to keep him waiting." He smiled coldly, as if by habit.

Now Olivia screamed at us, a blood curdling scream, "Now you'll get what you deserve you sons-of-bitches," As she screamed at us, she turned her back to the Tramp, staring at us like a woman gone crazy. I knew, and without reflection I hit her a hard, open-handed blow across the face, and she staggered backward toward the tramp as if she would fall, but at the last moment, almost upon him, she pivoted and stood straight as an arrow, and the S4 pistol went from his hand to hers faster than the eye could follow. She pulled the trigger and he died.

I slept on the floor on the rug by her bed that night. It was a rug hand woven in the desert hundreds of years before. We talked softly about weaving, our childhood, places we had traveled and also about the Silver Shuttle. We had designed the shuttle—a little, fat silver rocket—so that it would fly low down river, following the river to cross the fissure out of Missouri at a place where the volcanic action was so intense with heat and rising gases and covered so broad an area that flying through it almost at ground level might assure us safety from detection. Then by instruments we would land blind. Only the satellite, my development of the heat shielding mechanism and Gordon's equations and craftsmanship made it possible.

We had built a wooden raft for transporting it the few miles down river to the launching sight.

Olivia said it all sounded fine but that the future wasn't of much value. I asked her why. She said the best future was the present, and that Gordon was mixed up in fretting over something that was going to happen in 40 days when he had already done all he could in preparation. He could be learning something, she said, and enjoying it too. She brought up Mark Twain again and again, and how he wrote about the beautiful river flowing below us, and how he used that river to express truth. She said Mark Twain tried very hard. I said I was sorry I hadn't read more of his books, that I didn't know more about him. She said that really it wasn't necessary to know too much in that way, that one sentence could be enough. Soon I was to learn what she meant. Sooner than I thought.

At breakfast time she was sitting at the table in the long living area doing nothing. She was very still in the dawn light.

"I'm going to do some exercises I am accustomed to doing," she said. "If you would like to join me, you are welcome. Tell Jenna and Gordon to come too if they wish." She disappeared into her room without another word. I was apprehensive. I told Jenna, and she said that it would put her behind in her sewing, but that she would come for a little while, besides, she said, it would be good to move around a bit. I told Gordon. As usual he seemed not to care what the rest of us did.

"I don't need exercise," he said. "And another thing, I don't think I like that woman."

From here, time took a different turn and forty days and forty nights passed like a thousand years in the snap of the finger. There was no breakfast that day and no lunch, we skipped dinner too; Jenna, Olivia and I ate nothing for five days and continued the exercises, which Olivia called "work," stopping to sleep at one or two in the morning. Gordon came in at first and we always welcomed him to sit with us; we would stop what we were doing and try to make him feel comfortable, but Gordon wasn't interested in feeling at ease, he simply wanted us to be as he understood us, to worry with him, to be available for his needs, whether to complain or have a meal or discuss the theories of past and future which we had discussed countless times before.

And yet in what we were doing I felt that theory was dissolved in practice and that I was going somewhere inside and involved deeply in the time I was in. I felt alive, and Jenna, well, Jenna began to glow; a rather slow and tentative woman, she became light and limber and seemed to glide when she walked. Her smile could light a room. And she became herself, more loving, no longer the victim; though in his worry and waiting Gordon was more the aggressor toward her. And yet, it was not easy. There were times that I doubted the tall woman, or was it Olivia, and times I even wished she would disappear and give me rest, but she was relentless in her giving. It is not words, she told us, it is adjusting the behavior toward the energy of inwardness; it is an experience that is deep and connected with eternity. The behavior often follows; it adjusts itself. I took myself to levels of concentration that would be unimaginable to me before, and Jenna too, led by the woman who seemed all soft and powerful sitting cross-legged by the great window.

Soon Gordon was becoming accustomed to our habits and looked forward to being with us at meals when we ate them, or in the mornings early when we chatted around the hearth of the fire. He talked of the Silver Shuttle and of all the possibilities that he foresaw for us on the other side of Missouri. He would often take out the propulsion module, which he kept in a leather bag, and check its parts or show it to us, and smile—nine more days he would say, seven more days. Olivia would often go back to some discussion of Mark Twain; she would use him to talk of anything, of nature, of inner states, and sunlight, of travels and far-away places, of humor and children and the desire to learn. I don't believe she really cared a whole lot about encouraging us to read Mark Twain, and yet, we were all loving him. I think she had read enough to know him, his good heart, and she liked the fact that his beloved Mississippi was sparkling below us, and that in a way we were sort of living in his town as his guests. Gordon in his half-sarcastic half-joking way asked Olivia if she were some kind of religious fanatic afraid of ending up in hell. She winked and said she'd kind of go along with Mark Twain when he said, "I don't like to commit myself about heaven and hell, you see I have friends in both places."

Gordon burst into laughter, brightly, like a young child and pushed the hat he was wearing to the back of his head. It became like that, Mark Twain was our inside joke, our friend, who brought sweetness and a smile with the mention of his name.

I became very lean, as did Jenna, who would look at me now with her deep, almond eyes in understanding, and no word would be spoken. Olivia was there, constant, taking us to our limits, pressing the cracks of each new boundary; the false within seemed to go, allowing the invisible world to unfold, and three days before the 40th day, she stopped and told us to rest, to eat, to walk in the yard, to sew and do things, clean and chores around the house. We knew it was time for that stopping. Jenna came up to me as I stood watching the river by the great window; she wore the golden shirt of palms she had made, "I love you," she said. "Whoever we are." And she kissed me softly.

The night before we were to leave in the Silver Shuttle Gordon was tense, excited, trying to get everything ready and in order. We all worked steadily. We had to switch the turret gun to automatic with the remote trigger and put the steel shutters in place over the windows. Gordon was to carry the propulsion mechanism and the rest of us various sets of specialized tools and testing equipment. We were all to carry weapons. Gordon kept saying that we had made it, that we had beat the Scalar Destruction of Dr. Brune. Olivia never responded to that in any way, and I knew that without effort, her patience, her will power, allowed her to be only where she was. Jenna and I were watchful of both sides of that coin of time, still settling the energy from that explosive journey inward.

Olivia, that night, left a small crack in the steel shutters through which the moon shone for a long time. She called me from the rug on the floor to her bed, and without a need then to go further, we slept in each other's arms until morning. She kissed me and smoothed my hair and brought me spring water before we dressed. She was younger than I was by a few years. I asked her, but what did it matter?

The house abandoned, we moved through the trees toward the raft hidden at the river's edge. We triggered the turret gun with the remote and it began to fire with that distinctive high-pitched rippling and it would fire for hours. We felt that the sound might draw to battle the Tramps or the Diseased in the area and give us a better chance of moving unmolested. Traveling the river's edge, it would be nightfall before we reached the raft.

It was just after nightfall when we threw back the white canvas and revealed the silver rocket, mounted, and glowing a little with the moon and the clear stars. We poled the log raft from the bank and caught the slow easy current out into to the wide Mississippi. Gordon leaned against the rocket, and the three of us sat cross-legged in a semi-circle. All of us were quiet, not really thinking I guess, just watching the water and the sky and feeling the fresh night air. It was something so unusual as if the injured part of Missouri had been healed, or was healing, and we rode a new inward current that was exaggerated in our hearts and very real. I looked into Jenna's eyes and into Olivia's eyes and a soft energy went through me; I leaned back against my hands and turned my head upward and took the most amazing breath, when I saw to my left the cloud like substance fill the sky in the distance. I saw everything: Gordon had his head under the shuttle checking the mounts, Jenna and Olivia sat up straight in an exaggerated way, Jenna following Olivia's lead, and I too straightened. Jenna and I looked at Olivia, into her eyes, solid into her eyes—our concentration was unequaled—and then Olivia smiled, true and beautiful and unending, and with a certain glitter she said, "Mark Twain," and all of us softened in that sweet unreasonable, wordless state that was deep beyond compare, "He danced on this river."

There was a click in the air, as if the click surrounded us, or a sensation, as if lightning had struck without light and without thunder—I did not hear, I knew it—we became a sort of a tender dust, and I knew we were dead, but I was there and Olivia and Jenna close within me, or beside me leaning sweetly on my arms and shoulders and whatever substance we were was intertwined; and, unrushed, we had all the time that ever was. And for a moment Gordon was in the distance, undefined, looking for something, as if he had lost the Silver Shuttle; he was struggling mightily; and though I felt I could, I didn't need to see what he was seeing. He seemed in a way of coming toward us, little by little.

And there was Mark Twain, dapper and demure, dressed in white. Undead, we smiled at Mr. Twain, who, smiling too, gallantly indicated it all for us, by sweeping his arm toward the vastness.

Indian Ponies

We rode hell bent for leather, my friends from town and my cousins from the farm next door. We rode strong, swift-running horses and we rode for the excitement and the peace of the horses and the rolling, green fields. My cousins had a bunch of horses. One was a half thoroughbred paint named Honey. A couple of the older boys were always on her. But I watched as she laid back her ears and flew across the fields, stretching out, sure of foot, never a stumble over dangerous ground: death dealing groundhog holes, steel-like branches of Osage orange, or the bleached white bones of a cow long dead. Honey could dip low on the run. She seemed to be at her most romantic on the run, in her graceful, heaving curves between the trees flashing by, through a gap in the fence, leading us to our next field of adventure.

We had bawdy names for all the gates and gaps we passed through, comic phrases, unrepeatable at home. We were inspired and secure at heart when hanging on to the mane of a horse at a dead run. Our horses sailed as swift as a pirate ship on the black and white celluloid sea with Captain Blood at the helm; we were as daring as Lord Johnnie.

We named them. There was Satan, for good reason, Honey, Pretty Thing, Blade, and Miss Minerva named by a little sister, but we kept the name anyway. There were paints, bays, chestnuts, buckskins, and Sport the big Appaloosa. They loved to run. Nothing in our lives was as fast as the horses we rode. We could imagine nothing faster. Cars didn't count; we weren't old enough to drive them, and cars were cold and heartless and had to stick to the roads—entirely boring.

Bareback always, we would take off at a nod. In a heartbeat, Satan and Pretty Thing would be side by side at a dead run, and my cousin Timmy, riding behind me, would jump from Satan to Pretty Thing and back, getting a hand from my cousin Edmund who was riding her. No one ever fell. We were Tecumseh and Chief Joseph. We were the Lone Ranger and Lash Larue. We were knight errants protecting beauty. The drum of the ground thumped under the hooves. Our focus and concentration were impeccable. The horses disregarded our daring; ears laid back, they took themselves for a run, the leather reins loose and swinging against their necks.

We would ride into the woods at full tilt and swing from the tree limbs letting the horse run out from under us. No bones were ever broken. And if we fell into walnuts with rotting shells, the walnut stain would ruin a shirt if we had one on, or give our skin battle marks that happily took weeks to wear away.

We liked to think of the Indians. When I was very small, my mother read Blackfoot teaching stories and myths to me at bedtime. That could be a pretty rough way to be led into sleep, as the stories often taught lessons in a rather fearful manner. Rascally, cantankerous, death-dealing "Old Man" was often the protagonist. Yet we liked the beautiful illustrations by Remington and the romance when the Indian princess appeared. Chief War Eagle told the ancient stories of his tribe, lit by the flames of the open fire in his teepee on starry moonlit nights, passing them down to the young ones.

The farm was as quiet as a meadow at the beginnings of time. Birds would whistle, the wind would sing, a dog would bark near home or way far off, a crow would caw caw caw over the distant shine of snow in the eye of winter. Spring brought yellow flowers, chestnut foals, shaggy calves, and baby rabbits, which were brought down laughingly by angels. School and work on the farm after school were in the mix. We lived in the bluegrass, young and tied to nothing.

My father was unusual, at times spontaneous you might call it, a romantic toward animals. He liked donkeys, birds, horses, and cattle, wildlife, the outdoors, all of it. One day when he was away with his work in the city, he called long distance and said that some Indian ponies would be arriving soon.

"What is an Indian pony?" I asked.

"They are wild horses from the West," he said. "These are from Colorado. I saw an ad in the Chicago paper, that they were being gathered up on the range, and if someone would buy them they would be saved. They are all wild. I got them cheaply. The government is looking for homes for them. They are sending a truckload. They are descended from the horses of the tribes."

We had plenty of horses for breeding. I had a horse to ride. We had cattle, peacocks, chickens, ducks, dogs, and the problems and pleasures of caring for them. Yet these Indian ponies were for my father. The romance of horses and the Western plains was in his heart.

Indian ponies! They were a fresh mystery for me.

Before the truck arrived, something changed in me. It was a focus, I guess, reining me in, stopping me for a deeper look. I was to get my license to drive in a week or so. My friend Jimmy got his license early. After school, he would drive out to my farm in his parents' green Pontiac to catch the horses for a ride. Yet, a little older now, we rode the horses over the farm a lot slower, just looking around, talking about life, not letting the horses run free for one of those wild rides across the fields.

Jimmy liked to tell me about a younger girl named Sharon from another school, and how they liked to drive around at night, going nowhere is particular. Her mother didn't know. Then it wasn't long before Jimmy said he wouldn't have time to ride horses after school, as he was going to pick up Sharon.

Olivia, my true love, said that we must be apart, that she was leaving for a semester's credit at an archeological dig; and, in her way of speaking, often taking in the whole of things, she said that I should live as if she might never return. In some generous manner, Olivia was speaking of my freedom to learn, to be with people freely. Soon after, Lorraine left me a note. I hesitated to tell Jimmy about the note, but finally I did as he was talking so much about Sharon. Lorraine, a year older than I was, had left a note in my locker asking if I might like a ride home after school one day. I had not told her yes, and it had been two weeks since she had asked. I wish I hadn't said anything to Jimmy. "Are you crazy," he shouted? "She's more than cool. Every guy in town wants to go out with her. She just broke up with an idiot from college. Wake up. Olivia is gone; she is not thinking of you." And he kept going on and on like that about Lorraine. Jimmy knew of the mystifying closeness, for so many years, of Olivia and me. Our relationship was otherworldly to him; he didn't understand it. To Jimmy, Olivia and I traveled strangely from one arcane passageway to another, sometimes together, sometimes apart.

"What is this Olivia deal?" Jimmy would ask. "I don't get her. I don't get you for that matter. I see you together and then I don't. You all act like some kind of guardian angels, not just plain old boy friend and girl-friend. Don't you ever fight?"

"I guess it is a kind of mystery, Jimmy, even to me."

"Sometimes I think you two are real," Jimmy said. "Sometimes I think you are just a thought worrying my brain."

"You got me, Jimmy, maybe we are both."

The Indian ponies just appeared. No one called to tell us they were coming. It was on a Sunday. I heard the big truck with wooden slats for racks come slowly up the avenue. I grabbed the phone and called Jimmy. "Hey, Jimmy, quick, the Indian ponies are here." My father was working in the city; my mother was in town getting supplies for the week; so it was up to me to get the horses settled.

It was a strange time for these Indian ponies to come, as I had been sitting alone reading in an old leather bound book that had always been on a table in the house somewhere, a book I had picked up but never opened. It was a collection of poems, put together because they were all about something deep in a person's psychology, or about the mysteries of the universe. It made me think about life, and I remember settling into it, and sort of forgetting where I was, and just going out into a feeling of the hugeness of life itself. In the past, I had thought of those mysteries—what life and love might be—but never so clearly. I was taken by a quatrain telling poetically of a man and woman having a picnic alone on a desert beneath a bough, and another that spoke of generosity and laughter and scattering that across the world as gold. How happy I imagined them to be! The arrival of the Indian ponies jerked me out of my thoughtfulness, but it took the walk to the barn to really shake the poems loose.

Jimmy must have driven at top speed, as he got to the barn while I was still talking to the truck drivers. I thought the men who delivered Indian ponies would be really top notch horseman, bringing in wild horses from the desert, but they weren't. They were just there to get the job done and leave, didn't know a thing about horses. There was a small paddock near the hay barn where we unloaded them onto a wooden ramp and into the field.

The horses spread out across the field, some running to the corners nervously and then across the field to another corner and back. There were twelve of them. None of them were actually ponies but the size of horses that you might see the Native American Indians ride in the movies. There was a mix of colors, and they were not all well proportioned. All of them were lean. There was a dark bay with white stockings and long legs, and a small boned chestnut, both gaunt from lack of food. Most of the horses pushed close against the fence and moved along it and broke out toward the center and crossed to another fence, looking for an avenue of escape. They were all fillies and mares, no stallion among them.

Strangely, there were two who stood in the center of the field. They didn't run with the rest. There was a beautiful white mare; she stood with her head held high and looked around, now and then glancing our way, unafraid. Behind the white mare, a buckskin mare with a black mane and tail shifted about nervously, looked into the distance and back at the white mare. The buckskin deferred to the white mare, watched her for direction. The buckskin was taller than the others. She shifted from side to side and neighed loudly, but she would not leave the calm, white mare.

We filled the water trough for them and moved away. I knew horses pretty well. It was clear the white and the buckskin had been handled, but how much?

"I think the white horse might be broken to ride," I said, "maybe the buckskin, too."

"How can we tell?" Jimmy asked.

"Let's get bridles and a bucket of feed."

The white horse knew what the bucket was. Her ears came forward to look at it. The buckskin stayed close by, moved around her, avoiding us. We walked the white mare into a corner, and I soon caught her, and I held her with my arms around her neck, and Jimmy slipped the reins over her head.

Jimmy held the reins, and I moved to her side.

"What are you going to do?" Jimmy was nervous. I was nervous, too, but I knew we could just jump away if things didn't go well. I told Jimmy to stand to the side and hold the reins. I put my hands on her back. I pushed down with my hands; I patted her back, and then I slapped it firmly. She was quiet. I jumped up with my chest against her side and slid back down. She didn't move. I jumped and laid myself across her back. My arms and head hung over her opposite side; again I slid back down. She was quiet. None of that seemed to bother her. "Here goes, Jimmy."

I was up. She was truly a beautiful mare, all white with a long, white mane, tale and forelock. I got her going, stopped her, turned her a few times. It was amazing; she was expertly broken to ride. How could a horse like that be among a group of cheap, wild horses from the West. It didn't make sense. It was as if she was rounded up by mistake. Maybe she had escaped from a ranch and had been running with wild horses. I couldn't figure it. She neck-reined. I could lay the rein softly against the side of her neck and she would turn on a dime.

Immediately, I thought a great deal of her; she felt like mine, and she seemed to care in some strange manner, to care for what she was doing, focused right there with the time she was in. I fancied that she liked me; she seemed to. I felt strength from her, something I had felt from other horses from time to time, but never like this, never so refined, nor as attentive, nor as settled into the action of the moment. I had been reading those deep poems in the old leather-bound book when the Indian horses arrived. I had seen the word "spirit" in a poem that made me shiver, stopped my mind from thinking. Riding her, something of the feeling of the poem, like a shiver, a tingle in the back of the neck, came over me again. I decided I would name her Spirit.

I rode Spirit while Jimmy walked, as we forced the buckskin into a corner. Soon Jimmy was up on her, which was another surprise about these supposedly wild, untouched horses. Both Jimmy and the buckskin were wild-eyed. The buckskin was what is called "green broke," meaning broken to let someone stay on but not well schooled in responding to the signals of the rider. It was lucky that Spirit was there for the buckskin to follow. There was nothing smooth about the buckskin. She had a ridge of bone prominent in her lean back and a back breaking trot and a drunken walk. Jimmy screamed profanities complaining of permanent damage.

"This wench is going to kill me," Jimmy screamed in pain. "She is a man hater, killing my dreams." And then he yelled louder. "But I like her." He did like her, and soon went to the barn for a saddle blanket that he strapped around her for a cushion. He would not stoop to use a saddle.

She was tall and lean mare with a black mane and

tail. Jimmy said she was as good looking as Sharon. He liked to ride her. He said he felt like an Indian in the desert. He didn't really care what damage the mare did to him, or how she felt about the situation, or if she would learn: no future, just ride.

"Let's name them," Jimmy said. "I'm calling the buckskin Babe. Come on, my baby. Or should I call her Sharon? What are you naming the white?"

I always liked Jimmy's bluster. He got us laughing.

"Spirit," I said.

"Boring," Jimmy said.

"You're probably right."

"Hey, why don't I come back later, and let's go riding tonight out on the road," Jimmy said. "We've never ridden out on that road."

"Let's ride now."

"I have to meet Sharon this afternoon. We're going to drive out to the river road spot." He winked and then closed his eyes as if he were enjoying something tasty. "Why don't you call Loraine and go somewhere. She's hot for you. Girls don't ask to drive you home for nothing."

"Come back later," I said. "We'll ride on the road."

The road was a four-lane interstate highway under construction. It was going across country east to west, right through our farm, passing a few hundred feet from our home. The dynamite shook the house. Workers had completed construction of two ends of the interstate and were now building the last section, joining the ends together right there in a big field in front of the house where we used to graze and ride our horses. Part of our farm was now on the other side of the road.

Night had fallen when Jimmy arrived, and there was no moon. We caught the horses. There was just enough starlight in a shifting cloud cover to let us find our way. We knew where the gates were and how to double back to get up on the roadway under construction. The roadway was graded with fill so that the roadbed sat high above the fields like a low bridge. The road had been graded flat, and the horses were walking on dirt that had been flattened out by the big machines. In the near dark, huge earth-moving machines, forty feet long with twelve-foot wheels, would suddenly loom next to us as giant shadows in the starlight. We rode the horses slowly. It was almost entirely dark. Spirit moved smoothly and Babe followed a half a length back. Jimmy and I were both a little nervous, so he started talking, but quietly. It was so silent out there.

"Hey, why don't you get with Lorraine. And remember that girl, Melissa? I saw the way she acted toward you that night at the dance. She is a hot ticket."

"Lorraine still goes with a guy in college," I said.

"They must have broken up."

"Yeah, maybe."

"There is no one who wouldn't want to spend a little time with Lorraine. Right? I mean, what about those legs?" Jimmy said.

"She runs track."

"Come on, get serious. It's time you got up close to someone like Lorraine. You're not getting any younger."

"Right."

"I mean, listen, Sharon is really good to me. She…"

"You ever like poetry?"

"Yeah, yeah, don't change the subject. There is plenty of poetry in English class."

"Hey, Lorraine is nice. Okay?" I said. "I don't know her very well. She's great looking, good smile, but can't a guy be in a different mood some days?"

"All right, all right, all right. What about poetry?"

"Not just poetry. Something different, something else going on in some of it."

Jimmy's voice seemed to be a little distant as his last "all right" faded. Clouds had come over the stars, and the night was pitch black. I couldn't see anything.

"I mean poetry which talks about our thoughts and what we are doing with them," I said. "There were these thoughts I saw. I was reading in this very old book...."

Jimmy said something way down below me that didn't fit. "We could double date," I thought I heard him say.

Then I realized I had very gradually been going up some sort of strange hill in the dark where I knew there was no hill. I had forgotten about the Indian horse I was riding. I had forgotten that she was making her way in the dark, too, and that she looked to me for her direction. We had only just met—the Indian pony and I. Suddenly, she was going straight up, as straight up as a horse could go and still walk. I had to hold on with my knees squeezed against her sides and my hands wrapped in her mane. I felt her picking her way upward through rubble as if on a mountainside after an avalanche.

"Whoa," I said softly and held back gently on the reins.

She was climbing a huge mass of waste, a black mountain of refuse, iron and rock and broken forms, and matting used to contain the casualties of dynamite, all pushed into a mountain by the tremendous dozers. It was so quiet and dark out there. She was steady under me; there was faith from both of us. I felt that shiver at the back of my neck, as if from the poem, as if from memory of life over the eons. She was an Indian pony, a white horse with a deep understanding of the moment. She loved me gently from the beginning, just off the truck from far away. She loved me because she was made of love, and because I was there. Her name was in the poem I read. Under me I could feel her steady hold on life. We ended our struggle with the ruin that would soon shore up the constant moan of a highway. In that silent moment high on the mountain of waste, so much was understood. It was so quiet and dark out there. She never flinched; she never faltered. She would have climbed forever.

The Light in the Distant Room

In the cool fall, red and gold, when the walnuts were dropping to roll in the pale grass, when they hit with a thump against the smokehouse roof; he was there in the blue light. He wanted to know; and he was willing to strive to learn it all. Why should he not think of wisdom? He felt like the wind. Red leaves flying from the trees. A solitary bird was speaking. To himself he said, I can be just like the wind.

He thought of Olivia. He thought of Mack. Then he could not think.

"Uncle Jones, where are you?" Down near the arbor with a lattice and a sharp saw? Not there. Where?

Johnny thought for a moment—a lion—and gracefully searched with his eyes for Uncle Jones. Out in the pasture near the white sycamore he saw his silver, long legged mare running the curve, her mane flashing high in the breeze. Johnny ran too—kicking and jumping, they sailed on by: charmed particles—one this way, one that—the race begun and won in a breath.

Near the greenhouse, where the light fluttered in the glass, by the steaming flowers he found Uncle Jones. He was repairing the door with a plank of yellow wood. He sat on the stone walk by his leather grip sack. The old tools shone in the sun like silver. With a plane he was shaving the edge of the board to make it true. With an ease of concentration he pushed the plane, and the yellow shaving curled out like a ringlet of sun blonde hair. Like Olivia's golden curls, Johnny thought, for her, I'll get one.

"How old are you getting to be?" Uncle Jones asked,

with that light he could bring to his eyes. He always asked that, every few days at least.

"Nine, seven, eleven to come, the next one better than the last of 'em," Johnny said. That's what he always says to me, Johnny thought; but he must be a hundred.

"You right about that," Uncle Jones said. He took the pipe from his mouth and tapped it on the stone walk. "The next one should always be better than the last one. You know why?"

"No," Johnny said, surprised at the new twist. "Why?"

"Cause that's the one you got." When Uncle Jones ate a ripe paw paw from our tall tree in the lavender garden, he said that too, thought Johnny. Lavender was the garden's name, with silver fruit branches and wild red roses, often all rain and sunlight.

Uncle Jones's mustache was curved and gray. He came from the mountains. He was tall and slender. He wore high boots, a dark flannel shirt and a vest. His old hat had a broad brim darkened from wear. There was a hole in the point of the crown. I won't ever say: Uncle Jones, there's a hole in your hat. You're right about that, Johnny, he would smile, if I did.

At sunset that same day the snow began to float down, a storm of white narcissus. It was a strange sky for the sun was making colors in the west and for a moment all the flakes were wild red roses. Johnny was waiting for one to fall in his hand when Mack slipped under the fence. Mack lived on the farm down the road at the horseshoe curve.

"The bull chased me," Mack said. "But I got away. I hit him with a clod right between the eyes." Mack spit over one shoulder and hiked his pants up with both hands. He walked up to Johnny and looked him straight in the eye. "Let's do something."

"The snow is red," Johnny said.

"Snow's white," Mack said. "Got any gum?"

"Nope," said Johnny. "Let's go find Uncle Jones." Johnny still held out his hand, and it was wet from the red snowflakes that were falling.

"I'd rather go start the tractor," Mack said.

"We promised we wouldn't."

"I don't care," Mack said.

"Besides it's boring. I'd rather do something different," Johnny said.

"We could back it up."

"We've done it," Johnny said. "Maybe Uncle Jones will tell us a story."

"He's boring," Mack said.

She ducked under the low limb of the golden rain tree by the garden gate. A branch hooked her soft, white cap and her blonde curls cascaded to the shoulders of her coat. She stood there surprised, as slender and as graceful as the limb that lifted her cap. And the snowflakes falling large and white again, began melting in her hair. Olivia! Johnny took an extra breath and with bright eyes, sunk his hands into his pockets. Mack took off running.

At Olivia's side Mack told her what was not true. "Johnny said we should go start the tractor, and he said he would go in the house and get some cookies and bring them down, and he said we should run on fast before his mother came out and not to wait for him."

When Olivia ran away with Mack, tears tried to well up in Johnny's eyes, and in his pockets he clenched his palms together. Why didn't she wait for me? He brushed his eye with the edge of his hand and tried to look into the falling snow for comfort. But the flakes appeared small and sharp and seemed no longer beautiful.

The trees had lost their edges in the sheets of night fall. Through the damp window Johnny watched the two of them, Olivia and Mack, fade and come again, coming along the gravel walk. Shadows fell across the cold. They came making footprints. She wasn't holding his hand. Mack was talking. He kicked the snow as he talked, probably telling her lies about the bull, Johnny thought.

"Hi, Johnny," Olivia said. At the kitchen door—the bright lights. He wished he were damp and cool like her.

"Where have you been?" Johnny's Mother smiled.

"Riding the pony," Mack said.

"Next time go with them and help them, Johnny. Take off your coats and have dinner with us if you like."

"Thank you, Mrs. Williams," Olivia said. She jiggled her arms out of the sleeves of her coat.

"What are you having?" Mack asked.

"I'll call your parents, and take you home when I take Uncle Jones home," Johnny's Mother said. At the big stove, she lifted the lid of a rich, steaming soup.

Down the long hall, over Olivia's shoulder, Johnny saw the glow of red fire. Olivia looked at Johnny with the edges of her eyes. Mack pulled at her arm.

"Race you down the hall," Mack said. He pushed her ahead and she ran, and he passed her, and Olivia laughed near the marble statue of the gentle woman with the blue urn, and she felt the warmth of the statue's elegant smile and the freshness of the stone dress when she brushed on by with her hand.

Mack and Olivia skidded in on an ancient rug from Asia. And there by the fire was Uncle Jones. They had forgotten about him. Mack's eyes widened. Uncle Jones made him nervous. He didn't know why. So he sauntered up to the fire and turned his back to it for a moment as if that warmth was what he had come for all along. Olivia said, "Hi, Uncle Jones."

"Race you. Let's go," Mack said to Olivia.

"How do you do, Olivia. Have you all been out in the snow?"

"Yes sir, we have."

"Race you. Let's go," Mack said. He swung Olivia by the arm.

"Wait," Olivia said without looking at Mack. She pulled her arm away with a quick turn of her shoulder, her open hand cutting downward, a deadly move from a darker place. Again, she softened. Her eyes remained on Uncle Jones. Uncle Jones had the look of a Captain resting from the sea. He leaned back. He sharpened a small knife, slowly against a stone. Olivia's long curls were red with the fire. "Would you tell us a story, Uncle Jones?" she asked.

"Johnny?" She turned to search for Johnny, but when she met his eyes in the doorway, she looked down.

Johnny looked down too. He wondered if Uncle Jones could see him; the room seemed so full of people. Did Uncle Jones know that he had almost cried? No, he couldn't know. "I'd like a story too, Uncle Jones," he said.

Uncle Jones smiled at them with that light in his eye. He put away the knife. Olivia sat down on the rug, and Johnny sat down, not too close. Quickly Mack was on the rug between them, but then, with a flourish of his arms, he jumped up again.

"I want to hear a story from a book, not another made up one," Mack said. "I know where a book is."

"You don't know any books here," Johnny said.

"Yes I do. I saw it. It has an Indian on the front." Mack ran down the hall, and they could hear his feet on the long, wooden stairway.

Johnny looked out of the corner of his eye at Olivia. Uncle Jones, who had been about to speak, saw Johnny's look and quietly began to busy himself with the poker and the hot coals of the fire.

"Why didn't you come down to the barn?" Olivia asked in a soft voice that she was sure Uncle Jones was too busy to hear.

"I don't know," Johnny said.

"Mack said it was because you were afraid to drive the tractor, and because you didn't like me."

"I've driven the tractor before," Johnny said. But then he felt tears might come if he tried to say more. So he just turned warm in his chest and blended with her curls.

"Mack is going to buy me a milkshake tomorrow after school."

"I never said I didn't like you," Johnny said. But it was too late. He was almost sure she didn't hear him, because at that moment Mack burst in with the book, dropped it in Uncle Jones's lap, and sat down between them.

Uncle Jones crossed his long legs and sat up a little straighter in the firelight. He held the book as he might have held a piece of wood that he was eyeing for its beauty and its use, or as he might have held a precious stone. He touched the cover with his finger tips and brushed them across it, exploring the surface for smoothness. He held it up for the children to see the front of it.

On the cover was a painting of a magnificent man, an Indian. Across his back was a dark green bow and a quiver of yellow arrows. His skin was as red as the blazing fire. His expression held great determination and strength. The eyes painted there were kind. Behind him spread a scene of waters and woodlands, a sunrise was blazing. Bright feathers hung from his hair. He was as beautiful and wild as nature herself. Their own fire shown upon him. Johnny took an extra breath. Mack tucked his legs under himself. Olivia spoke softly, "Who is that?"

Uncle Jones hesitated, and they looked anew. Then Uncle Jones studied the Indian as if what was painted was real. He put his finger on a word and pronounced the syllables slowly, "Te...cump...seh," he said. Mack bit his lip, now a little embarrassed at what he had done, but puzzled too that Uncle Jones had read the word. His mother had told him one time that the old man who worked for Johnny's parents wasn't as smart as Johnny said he was, that obviously he wasn't Johnny's uncle, and the old feller couldn't even read. But Mack had never been so sure about the old man. Could he read Indian?

Johnny's mother looked into the fire lit room from the high, white doorway. She smiled. "Dinner soon," she said. "Don't go away." Her face, her form held the youth of one who cares, and in her movement was grace, and her soft dress was flowing, red. She had auburn hair, soft hair like Olivia. One hand drifted easy to brush her cheek.

"Uncle Jones is going to read us a story," Johnny said.

"Oh," his Mother said. "He knows all the good stories." She knew Uncle Jones couldn't read. She stepped over near him. "What story is this, let me see." She took the book and smiled. "Yes, this is my book, I've read it so many times. It's my favorite, it really is. My grandmother gave it to me. You didn't know her. She was strong and happy. Since I know this book so well, why don't I read something from it?"

"Please do," said Olivia. And the fire seemed to glow more brightly.

"A Tribute to Tecumseh," she read the title.

Uncle Jones reads Indian, thought Mack.

And they stared at Johnny's mother, so striking in the firelight, so at ease in the firelight, and mysterious like Uncle Jones—beautiful, like the princess in a story, and truthful like the queen. Johnny glanced at Olivia. He couldn't get past her burning curls. Uncle Jones leaned back, easy, alert, interested in what he might hear.

The woman's voice came softly, strong and true, like the storytellers of old. Her eyes, clear and sure, told the children that this story was her own, that what it was—its depth—she was.

Her red dress lay like water against her skin. She read: "Tecumseh was a strong man, clear of eye, born under a special star, when a meteor sailed across the heavens. As a youth he learned to ride and speak and play games, and he listened to the wisdom of his elders with an eye that was creative and humane."

"What's a creative eye?" Mack broke in. "How could he hear with his eye?"

"That means that he listened very carefully, that he saw deeply into what he was told," Johnny's mother said. "Creative means that he could make something out of what he learned that was true and helpful within himself and for the life around him."

"Oh," Mack said.

"Tecumseh not only learned the ways of his own tribe, but he learned the ways of all the tribes. He visited them; he listened; he asked questions. He not only learned the crafts and the ways of nature, but he spent time with the medicine men and the holy men to learn what was known by them. He fasted and spent time alone."

"What's fasting?" Mack asked.

"Not eating," said Olivia.

"Why?" asked Mack.

"To clear his mind, wouldn't you think," Johnny's mother said.

"Tecumseh became a natural leader. Natural, because he had energy to spare, and because something began to develop deep within him that gave him understanding and the force to express it, even when it went against the traditions of the tribe. It was the Indian's custom and habit, as long as any of them could remember, to torture their enemies when they captured them. After a fierce battle, when Tecumseh was only twenty, he stood between his tribesmen and a captured enemy and eloquently spoke against the practice of torture. He called his fellows cowards to torment a helpless man. From that day the custom of torture was abandoned by his tribe."

"What did they do?" Mack asked.

"They put ants on them," Johnny said. "I saw it in a movie."

Olivia put her hand over her eyes and made a face.

"I saw on TV where they were torturing people somewhere else, the other day, in some country. How come?" Mack asked.

The logs fell, bright sparks, orange and red, rained upward.

Uncle Jones watched the faces of the children, but they thought he only watched the burning logs. Johnny's mother remained standing in the firelight. Any true man alone and capable of love would have loved her, for her, for what she was. Any child would have looked, and in that presence found comfort. In an older time it would have been understood that she too had listened to the stories of the wise. Riveted to their place at her feet, the children waited. She read:

"Tecumseh saw as a hope for his people that they not forget the lore of the woods, and that they keep their relationship with nature, a relationship which was at the very heart of truth and the spirit and force of the universe, as a lifestyle and as the inward state of their being."

"I don't get that," Mack said.

"I do, sort of," said Olivia.

"Yeah, sort of," Johnny said.

"It's to know what is at the heart of things," Johnny's mother said. "To find the truth of life, no matter in what time you live. In the heart, what was true for Tecumseh is true for us. What do you think, Uncle Jones?"

"Yes ma'am, that's exactly right." His voice was low and clear. Uncle Jones, he's like her! The children felt it all like parallel movements of light—just that. Uncle Jones said no more. He knew the alchemy of her being. She read on.

"Tecumseh, when he became a powerful leader, spoke often to his people with great eloquence. And if they were not always strong enough to follow his wisdom, nor clear enough to see its value, still they loved him. And they did but what they could. He warned them against alcohol and the weed that weakens. He spoke of ways to bring clarity to their vision."

Mack lifted up on his knees. "What is the weed that weakens?"

"It was a drug they took," Johnny's mother said.

"They had drugs way back then?" Johnny asked.

"Even then," she said.

"Gosh," Olivia said. "That's strange. Why would

they want them way back then?"

"They say he was a prophet, that not only did he bring messages of truth to his people, but that he foresaw events before they happened. He predicted an earthquake that was so great the rivers and streams ran backward, and he told of the time when a meteor of great brilliance would flash across the sky. Tecumseh said: "Would that the red people could be as great as the conceptions of my mind when I think of the Great Spirit who rules over all."

Johnny's mother slowly closed the book. She waited to see if Uncle Jones would like to speak. The children were silent. Uncle Jones had only one eye on the fire. There was a hush over the room, a hush as deep and as truly beautiful as in any forest or lodge or painted tent of long ago—at night when there was firelight—entwined among the dreams of those gathered to tell stories of the rain, or of the ruins, or of the waves that carried them on.

"I'll get dinner," Johnny's mother said. Her voice was soft. "Tell them about Tecumseh, Uncle Jones." She lifted her head and seemed to breathe the firelight. She then turned and like the shadow of a gazelle was gone from the room.

Johnny felt his eyes want to fill with tears, because of everything: his mother, the fire, the Indian, the old hat by the chair, Olivia's curls; he breathed her. She looked down at her hands, and she could not think. But finally, the firelight on her hands made her remember by the green tree the red snow when it fell. Mack had his arms around his knees and was staring upward to the ceiling.

Uncle Jones let them be for a few moments, and then he leaned forward as if to tell a secret, a secret that could not be forgotten. It was almost as if they could see his quiver of yellow arrows and the wood of his long, green bow.

"You know children, if old Tecumseh were here now, right here with us, he'd be a good friend of mine."

"You know about Tecumseh, Uncle Jones?" Olivia asked.

"Of course I do. More than you know, child. Why I know people right now, on this earth, that follow in his footsteps."

"Who is that?" Mack asked.

"Why you were just looking at her. The very woman who was reading to us from that book."

Mack looked toward the kitchen light where she had disappeared. His eyes kept searching there.

"My Mom?" Johnny was incredulous. "You mean my Mom?"

"That's who for sure," said Uncle Jones in a tender voice to impart that great truth. "And there are others too. And it could be that the three of you will grow up in that same mold, and you will be brave and the world will be happier because of you. But you have to work at it some."

And the firelight shown on the wonder in the faces of three young warriors, faces transformed, clear, finer than before, intent.

"I would like to be like Tecumseh," Johnny said.

"I will be a lady Tecumseh," Olivia said. "I will grow up beautiful like your mom, Johnny, and I will learn all about everything."

Mack pulled his knees closer into his chest and tried to make himself small. He didn't want to be seen. He looked at the logs by the fire to try to quiet his heart from beating so fast. And he struggled to keep the tears from his eyes.

Uncle Jones waited, but he didn't wait too long.

"How about you, Mack?"

Mack's voice came out very faint. "I don't think I could," Mack said. He looked down at the floor, his long brown lashes rising and falling over his eyes.

"Could Johnny?" Uncle Jones asked softly.

"Yeah, Johnny could," Mack said. He didn't raise his eyes.

"Could Olivia?"

"Yeah, she could."

"You could," Uncle Jones said.

"I could?" Mack said in a voice filled with hope. He lifted his eyes. "Do you really think so?"

"I know so," said Uncle Jones. Brightness returned to Mack's face, but tears welled up in his eyes. He crossed his legs under him.

"How do you know?"

"How old am I," Uncle Jones asked?

"Maybe a hundred."

"Almost a hundred. I've been around a long time, and I know the type. And you're just it. Why I imagine you could be just like Tecumseh, and help the world coming and going."

"Sure you could," Johnny said.

"Uncle Jones knows," Olivia said.

Mack smiled an inward smile; his eyes slowly closed. His expression was generous, calm, final in that time. As surely as they had closed, his eyes snapped open. He rocked forward and backward, bursting to find something to do with his hands.

"I smell cooking," Uncle Jones said. He lightly slapped his knees with his hands, and then lifted his broad hat from the hearth.

All three children bounded to their feet, but hesitated…, uncertain, tentative, as if they had awakened from another world into an unfamiliar room. Johnny felt the yellow shaving in his pocket as a vision, as Olivia's golden curls. She lifted her eyes, but only as shining windows inward; she noticed nothing. Mack stared into the fire for a long moment as if stunned by the light, then turned slowly to Olivia and whispered, "I think Johnny likes you." For another long moment Mack seemed struck by his thoughts; he then bolted to the doorway, leaving Johnny and Olivia behind, and he knew, together.

"Race you," Mack said. "Let's go." And down the long hall toward Johnny's mother he ran, thoughtless of who might follow, on his own journey, alone, toward the light in the distant room.

Made in the USA
Columbia, SC
24 May 2018